AF434922

Zoar and Geneva

ANDERS A HOLMQUIST

ZOAR AND GENEVA

BOOK I

Adopted Homes

What is Earth but the home of humankind?

—Bishop Harvey Greenacre, Year 15 in Exile

CHAPTER I

When one considers the war between Next Frontier and Exosphere, the most important question will always be: What brought Zoar to such a state that we regressed to warfare, a brutal phenomenon once thought left in dust 1500 years ago?
—From "Why Now?" by Tobin Gorokhov

Next to the wide window in the orbital elevator's lounge compartment, Captain Brooklyn Kobayashi stood straight shouldered in her off-duty uniform of gold, orange, and red stars on black. The elevator ascended from a mountain not far from Sequoia, Zoar's capital. From where she stood, Kobayashi was just able to make out the namesake tree rising from the city center, a red, needle-thin spire amid the silver city. If she were to cross through the passenger level to the dining compartment on the other side, she would see Ponderosa and the evergreen forest that surrounded it. East between the two cities lay rolling hills of gold. To the west one could see the extent of the Cuscos Range. The sun set as the elevator rose from the midst of these tallest mountains on Zoar, casting an orange hue over the unclouded spaces and pink on the clouds themselves. It was an open, refreshing sight.

The lounge behind Kobayashi was confined and the air recycled. Civilians sat in soft couches with elaborately carved wood frames, chatting or scrolling through the news or stocks on their tactile handhelds, just as they had when she entered the lounge. Their clothes were smooth and sleek. One or two had brought their holo-displays from their sleeping compartments, but most preferred the privacy and portability of tactiles in public.

The elevator was a smoother (albeit longer) ride than a shuttle could give. More than that, one could watch the world shrink and with it the scars of war. By the time the initial acceleration ended and the harness light was off, the shattered husks of buildings were indistinguishable from the silver and matte of the rest of the city. If one knew where to look (and Kobayashi did) they would see a dent in Sequoia, where the heaviest fighting had taken place. It was in the western portion of the city and most of the destroyed buildings had still not been replaced. Kobayashi didn't look for the dent. While she gazed over the convergence of the green forest and gold fields, she heard someone approach her from behind.

"Quite the view, isn't it?"

Kobayashi glanced to her right. The speaker was a man holding a martini, complete with a green olive—a mark of wealth beyond the elevator ride itself, as the olive had proven a tricky transplant throughout Zoar. She looked forward again. "Yes, it is."

"You coming off leave?" He took the olive out of his drink and ate it.

"Yes."

"You chose the right way to travel. There's nothing like taking the elevator."

Kobayashi shifted imperceptibly. "I suppose there isn't."

"Are you stationed on Gibraltar?"

Kobayashi shook her head once. "Selene."

"Ah."

Kobayashi watched the Cuscos shrink. They were a jagged range, almost entirely covered in snow that the setting sun gave a rosy tint, right down to a straight line of deep green. Already, these monumental peaks were reduced to nothing more than an average of their nooks and crannies, colors and textures. Even Mount Nepal, the highest of all the Cuscos, held no distinct character beyond its summit, which reached just over that of the mountains surrounding it.

"This is my third visit to Gibraltar. I was just promoted to chief of sales for my company." The man tipped back his martini, draining the rest of it, and set the glass on a nearby table. "We manufacture diamonds for industrial use."

"Oh?" Kobayashi tilted her head, focusing her eyes on a pair of fiery red dots that grew as they rose out of Sequoia. A shuttle on its way to Gibraltar Station, no doubt.

"Yep. Of course, there are always a few that we hold onto for their beauty."

"I have something in common with diamonds, you know." Kobayashi made eye contact with the man and he flashed a smile.

"I'd have to agree."

Kobayashi's lips twitched upward, and she coughed something between a laugh and a scoff as she turned away from the window. "We're not thinking of the same thing."

"So, you're beautiful and tough. All the better." The man continued to grin, arms crossed and shoulders relaxed as Kobayashi looked a little closer at him. Like everyone else in the carriage but herself, he was dressed in sleek business wear, the dark colors shimmering slightly as he moved. He was an inch or two taller than her and grey was just beginning to creep up his sideburns. She put him at thirty-five years old and someone to whom the war had always been an abstract concept. Maybe it hurt business at first, but ultimately his company was better for it now, five years after it began, two after it had ended. Kobayashi imagined that diamonds and their industrial uses were in high demand in building ships and weapons, as well as the current reconstruction efforts. Her eyes flicked briefly out the window to Sequoia where the city's damage was all but indistinguishable now.

She looked back at the man and smiled, holding out her hand. "Brooklyn Kobayashi. Sell me a diamond?"

Kobayashi awoke sweating under satin sheets, the man breathing slowly next to her. She didn't look at him as she slid off the bed, collecting her clothes and dressing quickly. At the door, she glanced back at him and stopped. He shifted slightly, the sheet sliding down his chest. A toned chest. A chest without scars. Kobayashi stepped out of the room, pulling her hair into a short ponytail as she did so. She walked down the dark, carpeted hallway, smoothing out her uniform. Her own sleeping compartment was on the other end of the elevator, but she encountered no one on the walk back. Once inside the small space, she reached into the storage area above the single bed and pulled down her pack. Setting it on the edge of the bed, she rummaged through it until she found her clear, plastic handheld tactile. She dropped the pack on the floor and tapped it. It scanned her face and her handprint and unlocked. White lettering at the top of the display notified her of an urgent directive from command.

It didn't matter. Kobayashi wouldn't be able to do anything until the elevator reached Gibraltar Station. She opened the message anyway.

DATE: 0303 HOURS JULY 23, 1031

COMMAND DIRECTIVE

PRIORITY ALPHA-TWO

FROM: THE DESK OF GENERAL REILLY, KELLY C., MARSHAL OF THE MARINE CORPS OF THE JOINT RENOVAMEN EXPLORATORY FORCES OF THE PLANET ZOAR AND ITS TERRITORIES

TO: CAPTAIN (NAVAL) CLAYTON, JAMES; CAPTAIN (MARINE) KOBAYASHI, BROOKLYN

CC: ADMIRAL VILLENEUVE, ACHILLES; COLONEL GRIGGS, HOLDEN

ALPHA PRIORITY ASSIGNMENT: TOP SECRET; ALL OTHER ORDERS RESCINDED.

REPORT TO ADMIRAL VILLENEUVE ABOARD GIBRALTAR STATION AT 0800 JULY 25 FOR BRIEFING.

Kobayashi slid the message off the screen and tossed the handheld onto the bed next to her. She leaned back against the wall, fingers laced behind her head. Alpha-Two: action. She wished she hadn't taken the elevator and its slow, fixed rate.

Maybe she should have been concerned about the implications of action, given what had happened during the war, but Kobayashi just wanted to be doing something.

For now, she was stuck on a space elevator for two days with a man who would pursue her for the rest of the journey. Kobayashi didn't even know his name. Jake? Jack? It didn't matter. She sighed and stood. She grabbed her pack and, stuffing the handheld back into it, tossed it back into the overhead compartment. She took a look around the room and left, making the walk back to the man's room. She pressed her hand against the wall, which pulsed a soft green. The door slid open and she stepped inside, pulling her hair out of its ponytail.

CHAPTER II

Fred struggled to breathe through the heat and smoke. His eyes watered, but somehow he found the release and the door burst open. Looking back through the smoke, he found Dr. Murdock. She wasn't moving. He looped his arms under hers and dragged her to the open hatch. He heaved and managed to get her over the lip before his arms gave out. She fell to the ground. Fred coughed and slid down inside the door as his head pounded. He hacked again and his lungs heaved. He let out a weak, throat-tearing yell. He forced himself up to his knees and dragged himself over the edge of the hatch.

He fell three feet onto the ground. Gasping and coughing in the fresh air, Fred scrambled to his feet and stumbled away from the pod, clutching his side. Pain surged through his left leg and he lost his footing in slick, rust colored grass. He fell sideways, landing heavily on his arm. He rolled onto his back, lungs still heaving. He was too tired to stand but he managed to prop himself up on his forearms.

Then he saw them; three men and two women staring down at him. They were all tall and dressed in clothing that looked like it was made from blue and green leaves. All five of the people were armed with spears. Axes hung by their sides. One of the men reached down and picked Fred up by his shirt.

"Who are you?" Fred asked in a raspy voice. Then, everything faded to black.

In the evening light with the treetops glistening, Shar'hre stood outside her *mah* with the *Tuluchur*. Hrintar, she reminded herself; he was to be more than a prophet to her. He was to be her man, the one that no one else would see. They stood close and yet she dared not look up into his eyes. Instead, she took in his red hair and beard, his strong posture and listened to his warm, even voice.

"Shar'hre, these are sent by the *Jeli'ahsh*," Hrintar said. "I trust you to protect and administer to them."

"They are *Telahren*?" Shar'hre asked, looking into his eyes for just a moment. "They fulfill your teachings?"

Hrintar smiled before replying. "Yes, but they must survive or Genit and his non-believers will deny it."

"I understand." Shar'hre hesitated. "Tuluchur—"

"Hrintar, *lanha*."

She nodded, but her gaze remained low. "Hrintar. The woman—I do not think I can save her." Hrintar looked at her in silence for a moment and Shar'hre hung her head. Hrintar reached out and lifted her chin so that their eyes met. Shar'hre shivered slightly.

"The will of the Jeli'ahsh may be for her to die," Hrintar said. "It does not please me, but you will do your best." He moved in closer and held her shoulders as he pressed his lips against her forehead. Shar'hre's entire body contracted. "If she dies, she will but return to the Jeli'ahsh sooner than They expected. At least one of Their messengers will survive." Hrintar stepped back from Shar'hre and she let her breath out. "Go in to them. I must return to the *Keem*."

She bowed her head. "As you wish. Hrintar." He smiled and turned around, starting down the path to Gid'Del. Shar'hre watched him until he disappeared around the bend. How was she to be his *fiyal*? How was any average person to love and uphold someone in a station such as his?

With these thoughts lingering, Shar'hre stepped back into the mah. The Telahrensh slept in swaying hammocks of yellow *yelnahn* leaves. The woman was covered in purple *pulnahn* leaves from her waist up. They would ease the pain of her burns, but there was little else Shar'hre could do but hope and pray. She approached the woman and picked up her hand.

"Be at peace, *Jeli'ah*." Shar'hre released her hand and turned to the man. He had not awoken yet, though they had been rescued nearly a day past. Shar'hre sat down on the edge of the hammock and looked at him. His hair, though short, was red and his skin clear and unblemished; he had no *hredahsh*. Gold stubble grew in patches on his face. Given enough time, it might fill in a full beard. Despite that, Shar'hre guessed that he had only a few summers more than her.

He had only minor burns. Her greater concern with him was the puncture wound and his breathing. A rod of some kind of metal had gone all the way through his thigh. The damage was extensive, but relatively minor. He would recover, though it would be some time before he could walk without pain. Thinking of this, Shar'hre pulled his leafy tunic up to check the dressing. She peeled it back slowly. Blood did not flow out; the *weday* layering was working. Shar'hre tightened the dressing and pulled the man's tunic back down. As for his breathing, it was easier now, but she had seen what thick smoke could do to someone and she knew no long-term remedies.

She sat with him for a while, watching his chest rise and fall, shallowly now, shuddering the next.

She did not know what she had expected the Telahren to be, but she had not expected them to be so fragile, so much like the Meltesh. Still more surprising was how short they were. Nothing in Hrintar's teachings nor those of any Tuluchur before him said what the Jeli'ahsh looked like. Shar'hre had always imagined that they would all be handsome and tall and strong, a step above the Meltesh. Perhaps even immortal or untouchable. But here this man was before her, tangible and injured. He was not particularly handsome, nor did he appear strong. In fact, he looked weaker than any man she had yet met in her life.

But Shar'hre was not so arrogant as to believe all her imaginations of the Telahren to be truth. Life took its turns and that was all she could readily expect. Who was she to speak to spiritual matters? If the Jeli'ahsh and their Telahren did not have the strength that Meltesh had, they would have skill or knowledge beyond that of the Meltesh to make such strength unnecessary. Perhaps even that same knowledge that the Meltesh had lost when they arrived on Galjain a millennium ago.

Shar'hre looked at the man's face. When he awoke, perhaps she would learn more.

CHAPTER III

Cynics will say that it was the greed of corporate leadership and the complacency and stupidity of the common worker, that civil war was inevitable; that man is now and forever a brutal animal. This is a seductive and simple conclusion, but it begs the question: what of the dozens of generations of Renovamen who went without war?
—From "Why Now?" by Tobin Gorokhov

Kobayashi sat in a bright white hallway outside a door that was as white as the walls. Her navy-blue dress uniform was perfectly crisp, and her cover rested between her knees. Her pack rested on the ground beside her. She sat straight up and down, eyes fixed forward. She was fifteen minutes early to her meeting with Admiral Villeneuve and Captain Clayton. The moment the elevator docked at 0700 she had stepped through the airlock and made her way here, Beta Quadrant, Section S1, the heart of Gibraltar Station and of JREF Naval Administration. She had been fortunate to arrive so quickly; there had been no line to exit the elevator as most of the passengers weren't awake and most station personnel were already at work in their offices. After a few minutes of waiting, Kobayashi saw a man in dress whites and a monoplane pin on his collar approaching. She stood as he drew near, saluting stiffly.

The man returned the salute. "At ease." He extended his hand. "Captain Clayton. You must be Captain Kobayashi."

"Yes, sir." She shook his hand, but her posture remained stiff. Her eyes were the only part of her that moved, taking Clayton in fully. He stood an inch taller than her, with buzzed blond hair hidden under his cover. His uniform was immaculate, despite its color. He looked exactly as he had in his dossier and the headline interviews regarding his support for the Fleet Integration Project.

"Pleasure to meet you. I read your service record. Plenty of black ink."

Kobayashi gave a curt nod. "Likewise, captain. You're something of a hero among all the old Exos."

"And a villain among the NFs I imagine, but I like to think we've largely overcome our differences since the merger."

"Yes, sir. Wouldn't be much point in staying in the service, otherwise." Kobayashi paused for a moment, then made eye contact with Clayton. "Do you know what's going on, captain?"

Clayton shook his head. "I have no idea. I only just took command of *Trafalgar*. We were in the middle of shakedown for our maiden voyage when I received our orders."

"*Trafalgar*'s quite the ship. Not sure I'd want to take her into battle."

Clayton chuckled. "I guess that's the point. She's got teeth still. Just a thin skull." As Clayton finished his sentence, Kobayashi heard the door behind her swish open. A naval lieutenant stepped out and addressed them.

"Captains Clayton and Kobayashi? Admiral Villeneuve is ready for you."

"Thank you, lieutenant. After you, captain." Clayton gestured for Kobayashi to take the lead and she did so readily, grabbing her pack as she went. They walked through the secretary's small office space, white, just like the rest of the station and through another doorway into Villeneuve's office. Kobayashi hadn't been inside an admiral or general's office in a long time. The contrast between the white of these new JREF bases' operational areas and the comfortable decorations of the upper echelon of Command was drastic. The contrast between base and office had been worse during the war, but even now the oak desk, the soft carpet and taupe walls were so out of place as to set a veteran like herself ill at ease.

Admiral Villeneuve stood behind the desk, significantly taller than Kobayashi and Clayton. She put him at six-four. He had the frame of a soldier, but he carried himself like most of the Admiralty: a middle-aged civilian. His skin was just beginning to loosen, and his tuft of white hair was thinning evenly on top of his head.

"Captains, thank you for coming. Please sit down." He indicated a pair of chairs in front of his desk. Kobayashi and Clayton approached and shook Villeneuve's outstretched hand. "We don't have much time for pleasantries. If it were up to me, I would've called this an Alpha-One Priority, but we all take orders from someone." He smiled slightly, shaking his head.

Clayton said nothing and Kobayashi found herself filling in the silence as she set her pack on the ground as she took a seat. "Just as well, sir. I was on the elevator when I received the orders and wouldn't have been able to report any earlier regardless of priority status."

"Right. Well, best get on with it." Villeneuve tapped a few keys on his desk and a holographic projection of a planet sprang up onto the desk. At first, Kobayashi thought it was Zoar, but it didn't take long for her to realize that none of the continents were the right shape. "This is Geneva," Villeneuve said. "Our first viable colony planet. Top secret classification until the survey team comes back. Problem is, the survey team isn't coming back."

Clayton looked up sharply at Villeneuve. "Why not?"

"The ship, *Erikson*, was destroyed. When it stopped transmitting data back to Zoar, we sent a covert ops team to investigate. I think you're both familiar with the team. They were known as the Presidents during the war."

"Yes, sir." Kobayashi nodded shortly. She'd fought the Presidents on two separate occasions during the war. They were efficient and quiet. Deadly. Kobayashi glanced at Clayton who was nodding slowly, stroking his chin.

"When they arrived, they found a ... vessel in orbit. It seemed dead in the water, so they boarded it to investigate. Only two of the team made it back to the shuttle before the alien ship's systems powered up. The shuttle was forced to disengage, and the alien ship jumped out of the system."

While Kobayashi processed the implications of an unidentified space vessel, Clayton spoke. "I take it that *Trafalgar* is being sent to investigate further. And Captain Kobayashi will be hitching a ride?"

Villeneuve nodded. "A little more to it than that. Both the new Nelson-class ships are being sent to Geneva, along with the *Tovey*, under my command. We're going to rendezvous with the Presidents at Com Station G-4. Captain Kobayashi, you are being assigned to lead the marine contingent on *Trafalgar*. It's a single platoon, with one special operations team. It's a mixed platoon and a mixed ship, so bear that in mind. You are also hereby promoted to major." He grinned and opened a drawer in his desk and pulled out a small wooden box that he offered to Kobayashi. She accepted it with raised eyebrows. "That bit was my idea. It'll make the paperwork a lot easier on all of us, given the classification of this mission."

"Yes, sir. What's going to be my team's purpose on this mission?"

"Reconnaissance and retrieval—of alien technology and the kidnapped Presidents—if possible."

Kobayashi leaned back slightly in her chair, nodding curtly. She didn't know why they'd picked her. She'd been a desk jockey for a great deal of the war—she only got into combat in the last year of the war. She'd run a few torch-and-run ops during that time, but there had to be more experienced officers than her. She didn't care. This was an opportunity to get out of her cubicle on Selene.

"Yes, sir."

Villeneuve smiled and leaned back in his chair, kicking a foot up to rest on the opposite knee. "Good. We want to get this show on the road before week's end." He looked at Clayton. "Captain, from here on out, Major Kobayashi reports directly to you. I want *Trafalgar* ready to go as soon as possible."

"Aye, sir."

"Any questions?"

Kobayashi glanced at Clayton who shook his head firmly.

"Alright then. You're dismissed."

Kobayashi stood and saluted Villenueve. He returned it from his seat. Kobayashi shouldered her pack and turned to exit the room, Clayton right behind her. Outside in the white hallway, Clayton walked up alongside Kobayashi.

"You can report aboard *Trafalgar* whenever you're ready, major. I'll make sure my operations division gets you quarters."

"Yes, sir. I'll head straight there. I don't have any business on the station, and I'd rather drop my pack off sooner than later."

"Why don't you walk with me then, major? I don't have any business of my own on the station. The ship's docked in Alpha Quadrant dry dock, so we'll probably want to take the tram."

Kobayashi nodded. "Lead the way, sir."

Clayton started down the hallway at a brisk pace and Kobayashi walked next to him silently. There was little change in decoration as they walked—the occasional bench, grey doors set seamlessly into the wall. Signs suspended five feet above their heads gave directions to different sections and quadrants of the station: the tram, security offices, bathrooms. Once in a while they passed active-duty soldiers in black or white who stopped and saluted as they passed.

Fortunately, being at the center of the station, the tram stop wasn't too far away. It wasn't long before they reached it, just as the decelerating tram slid into view. The grey tram itself sat in black grooves in the floor and ceiling. Red and yellow hash marks marked the danger zones next to the track. While it broke up the Navy's preferred color scheme, it didn't make it any more pleasant. A small damage control station, manned by two enlisted personnel, jutted out into the hallway, but otherwise nothing broke the monotony of white.

The tram whirred to a stop and the doors slid open. A few officers and enlisted disembarked and Kobayashi and Clayton broke into a half jog to catch the tram before the doors closed again. Inside, like outside, just about everything was white. The walls, the floors, and the benches were seamless, except for the overhead rails for standing passengers. Those were stainless steel. The modern Navy knew at least that painting some things was a waste of time. But there could still be a whole lot less white. If it was purity Integrated Command wanted to imply, they weren't convincing anyone.

Kobayashi and Clayton settled into their seats on the tram and Kobayashi fished her tactile out of her pocket. She unlocked it and found the file containing the reports on the officers and enlisted now under her command. Forty in total: four officers, two of whom were pilots. She recognized none of them, but one of the noncoms, the senior sergeant for the platoon, she recognized: Fegan. He'd served under her during her combat tour during the war. He'd been promoted to sergeant major since. She nodded thoughtfully.

"Any initial thoughts?" Kobayashi looked up at Clayton, who gestured at her tactile. "On your team."

She nodded. "A few. I served with Sergeant Major Fegan during the war. Quick. An excellent sergeant. He commands respect and he's likeable. That'll be good for unit cohesion."

"Sounds like command chose well. Any other thoughts?"

Kobayashi tapped the tactile on her knee and looked over at Clayton. "I'm concerned about how green the pilots are. Only my XO and the spec-ops leader have combat experience."

"Understandable. But we're all green at one time or another."

Kobayashi nodded slowly. "Another thing, captain."

"Yes?"

"If I'm going to be running recon ops, I want people who know a thing or two about covert operations. The two Presidents who made it out—I know they're Navy personnel, but I think they'll be of greater benefit with my marines. Beyond being a ground force, they're going to be angry about the rest of their team. I can channel that."

Clayton nodded, stroking his chin. He replied after a moment. "I'll consider it."

"Understood, sir." Kobayashi nodded again. She looked back down at her tactile but didn't get any further than that before Clayton spoke again.

"Ah. we've reached the docks." The tram came to a stop for a moment, while the airlock vented atmosphere back into the station.

As the tram started off again, Kobayashi looked up and out the window. Instead of seamless white, she saw steel girders and pockets of black space. The girders reached far out into the blackness. Long, cylindrical ships hung evenly spaced within the girders. Smaller maintenance craft floated between the ships, too small to make out details. The larger ships had no real details to speak of, aside from variations in size, but as Kobayashi watched, that began to change. More experimental designs began to appear as they went further out. For the most part, it seemed that a variety of shapes were stuck directly to the sides of basic box or cylinder design. The color on some of the hulls changed as well but Kobayashi didn't know if there was any practical reason for this, or if some captains were simply vain enough to want to look like they commanded a ship of azure or gold.

"There she is—*Trafalgar*. First Nelson-class off the line. I think her sister, the *Nile*, is behind us." Clayton pointed out the window and to the right. Kobayashi followed his finger to the familiar ship. She'd only seen it before in the news, where it was touted as the most advanced ship to be built since the war. Its design wasn't much different from the typical warship: long, cylindrical and packing serious heat but it did vary from the typical cylindrical shape in two significant ways. Both ends tapered to smooth noses, like those used in atmospheric planes. The stern trended down according to the ship's current orientation, while the bow terminated higher. The second difference was far more significant.

Attached to the ship's port side was a clear bubble that showed off its white, naval interior. This was the command bridge, jutting out into space, far more exposed than the central hubs buried in the depths of most ships. An easy target and as such, a considerable motivation to avoid danger. Although there was a shell that could be extended around it, it remained the most fragile part of the ship. The ship could otherwise take a serious beating, having been built with two airtight hulls connected by honeycombed girders. As long as the bridge avoided damage, the ship would weather conventional warfare well.

Kobayashi looked away from the ship and focused on Clayton. "Why send the two most vulnerable and valuable ships in the fleet to investigate something so dangerous?"

The corners of Clayton's mouth turned down and his eyebrows drew closer together. "I've wondered the same thing, major. My guess is that they wanted Captain Amin and myself and that it was simpler to assign the ships we currently command than to make personnel changes. I've only just begun to settle in with my senior staff and maybe Command is aware of that."

Kobayashi shook her head. "But I was transferred to command your marine detachment. If we're supposed to be on the front line, you'd think they'd want us to have a similar level of familiarity."

Clayton smiled slightly. "You have a point, major. Maybe Command thinks that your platoon will adjust better than I would to a whole different ship or staff. I don't pretend to understand everything that comes down from on high. They have ... a different approach to operations than those of us in the field."

"That's one way of putting it."

Clayton let out a long, steady breath. "Aye." There was a moment of silence and Kobayashi felt the tram decelerate. It glided to a full stop inside a steel-colored airlock which pressurized, and the tram continued on its way. Only a few moments later it slowed again, and the utilitarian grey of the dock's hangar came into view through the window. Hexagonal work craft, with their four long arms and a pair of forks at their base, took up most of the spaces in the hangar, but a number of personnel transports were docked nearer its center. Because these transports were used for both space and atmospheric travel, they were large, with cylindrical fuselages, windowed cockpits, and wings that swept back. Some, Kobayashi knew, were large enough to ship an entire company, though most were only large enough to take a squad or two.

When the tram stopped and the doors opened, Kobayashi followed Clayton out onto the catwalk. They made their way down the stairs to the main level of the hangar, boots clanging as they went. It was about forty feet to the bottom. As they approached, Clayton glanced back at her.

"As you might imagine, I've got a lot of work to finalize before *Trafalgar*'s ready for launch. When we come aboard, I'll leave you in the capable hands of my chief operations officer. She'll get you quarters and familiarize you with the ship. Hell, if you've got any thoughts on a training schedule already, you can probably arrange time slots with her."

"Understood, sir." They were on the bottom floor now and Clayton led the way to one of the smaller personnel craft. Kobayashi cocked her head to the side when she realized that they were headed for it. It was smaller and sleeker than most. A *Coon*-class, sitting up at a twenty-degree angle on its landing stilts. She glanced at Clayton who grinned.

"*Trafalgar* has a couple. They spared no expense on the new flagship. I expect your marines will be using them pretty heavily." Kobayashi nodded and followed Clayton around to the back and up the steep ramp. As they walked past most of the seats, which lined either side of the craft, Clayton spoke again. "Can you fly, major?"

"No, sir."

"Since it's just the two of us, do you mind warming the copilot seat anyway?"

"Of course not, sir." Kobayashi followed Clayton into the cockpit and slid into the copilot's chair. She took in the buffet of switches above her head and the buttons and screen in front of her as she strapped in. Beside her, Clayton flipped switches and scrolled through diagnostics on his screen as if he'd been flying his entire life.

"I don't often get the chance to fly myself now. That's the problem with being promoted."

Kobayashi nodded, looking straight out at the hull of the dock. "Yes, sir."

Clayton chuckled. "You're a major now, Kobayashi. Be careful or you'll find yourself out of the action permanently."

"I was just thinking that it's ironic that I had to be promoted to get out from behind a desk, captain." Kobayashi didn't turn to look at him, but she could see him grinning as he reached up to flip one final switch.

"It is, isn't it?"

CHAPTER IV

Father sends me down the hill
To find the straightest staff 'fore the rain
He sees it coming,
He sees it rolling in a cloud.
On my way I see the wins all glide
'Before the storm, 'fore the storm' I stand and cry
'I see wins all going on,
'I see them going on always before the storm.'
—Traditional Meltesh Children's Song

Fred scrunched his eyes against the light. His throat burned sharply; he desperately needed a drink. His entire body ached too, but there was a different, more uncomfortable sensation in his left leg. He blinked, opening his eyes slowly, keenly aware of the brightness as he squinted at his leg. It was wrapped tightly in what seemed to be some kind of purple leaf. He reached down to touch the leaf and found that it was rubbery and slick. Fred flopped back and closed his eyes, noticing that the bed beneath him swayed; he was in a hammock of some kind.

After a moment he opened his eyes and pushed himself into a sitting position, finding he had to bend forward because of the hammock's shape. He glanced around the room, looking for the source of light. It seemed to come from everywhere, filtering through the ceiling and the walls, which were yellow and translucent. Black veins spiderwebbed across the canvas of the ceiling. Fred stared up at them, transfixed for a moment. He glanced around the room again and saw two other hammocks. In one, a face lay above a body wrapped in purple leaves like the bandage on his leg—Dr. Murdock.

"Doctor?" Fred croaked. His throat felt like it had just been slashed open. He needed water. Dr. Murdock did not respond. She must have been asleep. Fred made to sit up and swing his legs over the side of the hammock when a woman entered the room.

Fred snapped his attention to sound of her approach. She, like the others he'd seen before, was tall. Her skin was blotchy; patches of white skin stood out on her upper right arm and the left side of her neck. A line like that of an ocean meeting sand divided her face into two different shades diagonally across her nose. Her clothing was composed of long, blue and green leaves that overlapped like scales, covering her body from her shoulders down to her knees. Fred couldn't tell if it was a dress or if it was divided into separate garments.

The woman's face was angular and strong, with icy blue eyes and long black hair that was done in a single, thick braid. She carried a bowl in one hand and a jug in the other. They looked to be made of clay and Fred couldn't figure what was in either of them. As she approached, a strong, mouthwatering aroma wafted from one of the bowls. Fred glanced from the woman's face to the bowl. He licked his lips, suddenly aware of an ache in his stomach.

She reached him and sat on the edge of the hammock, offering him the jug. Fred looked into it, relieved to see what looked like water. He glanced at the bowl, which had what looked like an off-white porridge in it. Fred took the jug and lifted it to his lips. The first swallow was painful, but it grew easier. He tried to pace himself but found it difficult. He drained the last of the water and turned his attention to her.

"Thank you."

She smiled and he took the silence to study her. Now that she was closer, her eyes caught his attention. The whites were flawless porcelain, but oval slits split the frigid ice of her irises; her pupils were almost catlike. Fred suppressed a shudder and looked down. Who were these people? She came closer and sat on the edge of the hammock. He looked back at her, everywhere but in her eyes.

He noticed that her cheekbones were high and her jaw protruded. When he finally looked in her eyes again, the pupils had dilated some, becoming almost round.

She spoke, her voice deep and rich, yet distinctly feminine. Her voice reminded Fred of a long, distant roll of thunder. He didn't comprehend a word she said but she held the bowl toward him. Fred took it in his hands and raised it to his lips. The liquid seeped into his mouth, cold and sweet. He began to gulp it down, but the woman pulled the bowl firmly away from him, causing him to dribble soup or, more accurately, porridge on himself. He looked at her with wide eyes, cheeks full.

Then his teeth began to burn. Fred had never experienced anything like it and had to swallow hard to avoid spewing. Most of it coursed down his gullet, but he swallowed too fast. He coughed, first a small one, then more violently. The sensation in his teeth had receded, replaced by the tickle of incorrectly swallowed liquid.

The woman looked at Fred as he convulsed, her hand over her mouth, diagonal pupils still staring at him.

Once he had recovered from his coughing fit, the man pointed at the other hammock and spoke. His words were foreign to Shar'hre's ears, but she understood what he was asking. She looked down briefly, then shook her head and met his eyes.

"She will not survive much longer." The man looked from Shar'hre to the other Telahren and was silent for a moment. Then he swung his legs over the side, wincing and tried to stand. When Shar'hre realized what he was doing she moved to stop him, but it was too late. He collapsed on his weak leg, roaring in pain. Shar'hre helped him back into the hammock. His breathing was fast and heavy from the pain, but he sat in the hammock, refusing her attempts to guide him back to a laying position.

"You were sorely injured." Shar'hre knew the man did not understand but she hoped that her voice soothed him. "My name is

Shar'hre." He looked at her and she placed her hand on her chest. "Shar'hre."

The man frowned but nodded. He pointed to himself. "Fred." Then he pointed at her. "Shar'hre?" He formed her name carefully.

She smiled and nodded. "Yes. I am Shar'hre." She tapped her chest with her hand for added emphasis before touching his chest. "You are Hred?" He leaned away from her hand but nodded. Shar'hre pointed to the woman in the other hammock. "What is she called?"

Hred looked down and back up, speaking too softly for Shar'hre to understand. When he looked up, he spoke louder and more clearly. "Dorothy." He said something else but repeated those sounds.

"She is Dor-o-thee?" The name felt strange in her mouth. The syllables melded in an unnatural way, but Hred nodded. Shar'hre put a hand on his shoulder. "You have my sorrow." Hred looked down into his hands.

CHAPTER V

*A*n argument can be made that the loss of our faith as a people may have been a cause of the war; a cursory study of census records from the days of the Exodus through to now shows a steady decline in followers of any religion, but especially the main branches of Greenacrean philosophy. While it remains true that correlation is not the same as causation, I would argue that it is worth noting that Harvey Greenacre's teachings were unifying; nearly seventy percent of the final generation born in exile were followers of his Christian sect and the leaders of minor religions aboard the Mayflower (Buddhism, Islam, Judaism, ect.) respected and appreciated his writings on Earth and Exile, particularly People of the Book.
—From "Why Now?" by Tobin Gorokhov

Captain James Clayton walked down the corridor towards *Trafalgar's* forward storage compartment, looking down at his tactile. Thanks to the short timeline for launch, he found himself working every waking moment to ensure that they would be ready to go in the next few days. If it weren't for Dixon's dedication, he doubted they would be half as readd as he was. The ship's operations officer was a credit to the Fleet and all the proof Clayton needed that the merger could work. Would work. *Was* working. Tensions were still high, but if a former NF could serve an Exo—and serve him well—there was a very real chance that Zoar would heal from the war.

It was ambitious, Bear's integration program. Nowhere in his study of history had Clayton seen such a rift sealed. Then again, everything on Zoar necessitated a certain amount of skepticism when compared to Earth history. At no other time in history had humanity been as united as it was when it left Earth and settled on Zoar. Even when British pilgrims settled North America, there were French settlers to the north and Spanish to the south, to say nothing of the indigenous peoples. The Renovamen of Zoar were different. The common history that united them was the result of fifteen hundred years of political and cultural homogeneity, entirely uninfluenced by outside tribes or nations.

A door opened in front of Clayton but, lost in thought as he was, he didn't notice. Two hands stopped him in his tracks suddenly and he looked up to see a woman in black fatigues.

She snapped to and gave him a salute. "Sorry, sir. I didn't see you before I stepped out of the lift."

Clayton returned the salute. "At ease, lieutenant." Her shoulders dropped and she held her hands behind her back. "And don't worry about it," Clayton continued. "I wasn't looking where I was going." As the woman relaxed, he took her in. She was nondescript, of average build and height, but a brass bar on one side of her collar and the letters JFMC on the other set her apart as a marine officer. She was younger than he had thought at first too, clearly a greenhorn: one of Kobayashi's pilots. "Lieutenant Allred, right?"

Her eyes widened. "Yes, sir." She glanced down briefly. "I uh ..."

"Didn't expect me to know your name?" Allred nodded and Clayton smiled. "The marine contingent here is small; going through the officer's manifest was quick." He looked at her for a moment. "Do you have anywhere to be, lieutenant?"

"I was just headed to the mess for a quick bite. I have to report to Major Kobayashi at 0900 hours."

Clayton nodded. "I'm headed that direction as well. Walk with me."

"Yes, sir."

They continued on their way. "I want to apologize for the sudden transfer, lieutenant. We needed another pilot, and you were qualified and not already established in your assignment."

"It's no problem, captain. I was hoping to serve on a ship as it was." Her voice was light and friendly. She seemed a much warmer person than Kobayashi. Perhaps it was just naivety, but Clayton had a feeling they would be good foils for each other.

"Why's that?"

Allred smiled and gave a half-shrug. "The opportunity to go beyond Zoar and Selene. Same reason I suppose most people join the Navy."

"Why the marines for you then?"

Allred glanced down at her hands. "The war. Something made me think being a marine would keep me more grounded."

Clayton nodded and they continued in silence. It made sense to him, though he couldn't quite pin down why. He himself had started with Exosphere with a similar hope that when the light-speed barrier was broken and colonies were established, he would have the opportunity to visit them. That was before the war, of course. Still, he'd remained with the company even through its merger with Next Frontier and its development into the paramilitary Joint Renovamen Exploratory Fleet, more out of a sense of duty than continued hope for his dream to come true. It was coming true; he'd already been beyond the Hathor System and now he was being sent to their first potential colony planet. But he had to keep a level head.

He saw danger in the venture. Not just the unknown of exploring new worlds, but in uniting people who had shed each other's blood. He suspected that Director Bear saw it too, but one man at the top of it all could not handle every issue. It took others who saw the danger to manage it in smaller places. For that alone, disregarding the things he'd seen and done during the war, Clayton could not maintain the romantic view of space travel he had fostered in his youth. A verse came unbidden to his mind, and he found himself speaking it under his breath.

> *"'And the old man, tired, sat and watched the sunset.*
> *He was not so old, in truth, his hair still a dark canvas,*
> *But in short years he saw more,*
> *Hungered more,*
> *Gained some in his hunger,*

He felt Allred's eyes on him. "Sorry, sir, did you say something?"

He cleared his throat. "Just a favorite verse of my father's. It's from the 'Parable of the Aged.'" He paused for a moment. "Are you religious, lieutenant?"

He could feel Allred's hesitation before she replied. "Spiritual, at least, sir. My parents were religious, but ..." She paused, inhaled. "It's not easy to know what to believe."

Clayton nodded. "Neither is not knowing." Allred sighed beside Clayton, and he looked over at her. She looked straight ahead and he wondered what she was thinking. He didn't ask; he'd pried enough. They walked in silence the last few yards to the mess entrance. When they arrived and the doors opened to admit them, Clayton extended his hand to Allred. "Thank you for the conversation, lieutenant."

They shook hands. Hers was small, but her grip was firm. "Likewise, captain."

Kobayashi stood, hands resting on the conference room table. She leaned into it as she looked around the room. Sergeant Major Fegan and Kobayashi's junior officers were present, waiting for the meeting to begin. Only her XO was missing. Kobayashi glanced at the clock on the wall. 0928. Not late yet. No one spoke. Johansen prowled around the room. The two pilots, Allred and Holtz, stood restlessly. Fegan was the only one sitting. Leaning back and chewing on something, he looked more comfortable than anyone else. The clock ticked over to 0929 and the door into the room slid open.

Goldman hurried in, flashing a smile. "Everyone's here? Sorry for the wait." Seeing Kobayashi, he raised his arm in a salute.

She stood up straight and extended her hand. "Captain Goldman." They shook hands and turned toward the table.

He shook it and smiled again. "Pleased to meet you, Major."

Johansen stopped prowling around the room and approached the table and the others straightened up. Kobayashi nodded and looked around at them.

"To business," she said. "What's the status of the platoon?"

"Mithril squad is RTG, major," Johansen said. "Armor fitting will be done en route, but it should be finished in a week or so." Kobayashi nodded.

"Alpha and Bravo are ready to go as well, major. No fancy armor to fit them for, but ..." Goldman inclined his head to Johansen. "All your marines are combat ready." He looked at her, eyes narrowed slightly. "If that will be necessary."

All eyes were on Kobayashi. She gave a nod and placed her hands on the table. "Our mission is still classified. I will disclose details as protocol permits." She looked at the pilots. "Holtz, have you had time to go over our shuttles and munitions?"

"Yes, ma'am. All accounted for and in proper condition."

"Have you had the opportunity to bring Allred up to speed?"

He paused for a moment. "Not yet, ma'am."

"That's your next priority."

"Understood, ma'am."

Kobayashi looked from him to Allred. "You two might be pilots, but you're officers too. As such I'm assigning Allred to assist Johansen with Mithril. Holtz, you'll be with me and Alpha."

Both nodded their assent. "Yes, ma'am."

Kobayashi turned to Goldman. "As far as officers go, you're on your own with Bravo, but I'm assigning Sergeant Major Fegan as the squad's sergeant in addition to platoon sergeant."

"Understood, major."

"Good." Kobayashi looked down the table at Fegan. "Sergeant Major, any concerns?"

Fegan continued chewing. "Not a one, major. Just be sure you see the men soon yourself. They're jonesing to meet their new CO."

"All in short order. Captain Goldman, when have you been holding drill?"

"Zero six thirty, Major."

"Good. We'll keep with that. I understand facilities on the ship are limited, but I want each squad to find time three times a week to hit the mat and range, in addition to regular PT. Two days a week, I expect tactical studies. I will provide topics and materials for one of those days. We officers will meet twice a week to discuss any concerns or ideas about training as a group. Additionally, one day a week the platoon will mix for training beyond PT and another day for tactical exercises."

Holtz raised an eyebrow. "You expecting trouble, major?"

Fegan responded for Kobayashi. "Idle hands do the devil's work, sir."

Kobayashi nodded. "Precisely. We need to keep the men sharp as well as busy."

"Are you worried about ... interpersonal tension?" Allred asked, glancing from Kobayashi to Goldman, who was grinning again.

Kobayashi looked at Goldman as well. "I don't expect this to be easy, but the war's been over for a year now. I doubt anyone who wants to cause trouble is still around."

He held up his hands, grinning. "I know, I know—the only NF in the room. You don't have to worry about anything from me. I came to terms a long time ago. Even if I hadn't, I'd have to be pretty stupid to go up against Johansen." He laughed and dropped his hands. Holtz chuckled and Kobayashi saw Allred trying to hide a smile. Fegan raised an eyebrow and Johansen crossed her arms.

Kobayashi pushed herself away from the table. "Is there anything else you want to bring to my attention?" Everyone shook their heads. "Then you're dismissed." As the group shuffled towards the door, Kobayashi spoke again. "Captain Goldman, a moment."

"Of course, major." He stopped and turned back from the door as the rest of the officers filed out. When the doors slid shut, Kobayashi let out a silent breath. She pulled out a chair from the table and sat down.

"Have a seat, captain." Goldman inclined his head and pulled up a chair to Kobayashi's left. The smile on his face never left.

"What's on your mind, ma'am?"

"I want your honest thoughts on our people."

The smile evaporated. "Someone you don't trust?"

"I know none of you except Fegan. You've been over this platoon for nearly a month now."

"So, you don't trust any of us. Why ask me and not Fegan, then?"

Kobayashi pursed her lips. "Let's say I don't want to be biased. Or maybe I already asked him and this is a test."

Goldman grinned. "Why not both?" Kobayashi didn't smile and the grin shrunk. He leaned back. "Honestly, major, some of the enlisted seem less than happy. Doesn't seem to be split along pre-integration lines though. At least, not entirely. That's Alpha and Bravo. I can send you their names, so you can keep an eye on them."

Kobayashi nodded once. "And Mithril?"

Goldman raised his eyebrows in a bemused way and tossed up a hand. "Can't really get a read on them. I figured that after the war, special operations units might ease up a bit, especially newly formed ones. What do they have going on that they've got to keep a lid on during peace?"

"They keep their distance from the others?"

Goldman shook his head. "More like from me. I think Johansen trusts me less than you do. That having been said, some are more open than others." He paused for a moment, then leaned forward. "What's going on, major? *Trafalgar* wasn't supposed to launch for another two weeks. There's word going around that the *Nile* and the *Tovey* are rushing prep too. This isn't just some shakedown cruise."

"I'm not at liberty to say. Captain's orders." Goldman tilted his head, clearly waiting for more. Kobayashi held back a sigh and straightened her uniform cuffs. "It's big, Goldman. That's all you get."

Goldman leaned back in his chair, arms crossed. "First Johansen, now you. I'm starting to feel left out." He leaned forward and lowered his voice. "Those greenhorns, Holtz and Allred—you think they have secrets too?"

Kobayashi's mouth twitched. "You can go now, captain."

Goldman smiled and stood up. "Let me know if you find out. I'm always one for some good gossip." Kobayashi's lip twitched again as he made for the door.

"Would you want to know what the secret was?" she asked.

The door swished open and he looked back at her, face scrunched up in exaggerated thought. Then he shook his head. "Nah, it's more fun to speculate."

Clayton did not trust his first officer. Not that he would admit that to anyone; it was difficult enough to come to terms with it himself. The problem was that while he believed in Integration, something about Commander Spadt rubbed Clayton the wrong way. Not only was it hypocritical not to trust Spadt, it was unfounded. The man had done nothing to obstruct Clayton in running his ship. In fact, Spadt was almost as much of a boon as Lieutenant Commander Dixon, the chief operations officer. So why could he trust one NF and not the other?

Sitting at his desk several hours after *Trafalgar* left dry dock, Clayton wrestled with that question. He flicked through the reports on his desks without seeing them. There was nothing new anyway; everything was squared away and the launch had gone off without a hitch. Clayton closed the reports and the holographic display melted away. He looked around the cabin, realizing that it was the first opportunity he'd had to relax since the launch date had been moved up.

The cabin wasn't a huge space; approximately fifty square feet in addition to the bunk and head which adjoined the office space.

Still, the office alone was bigger than even the quarters his junior officers shared, crammed four apiece into two sets of bunks with barely three feet between them. Truly, by naval standards, Clayton's office was luxurious. His antique, oak desk sat facing a bookshelf and display case in which Clayton had set two replicas: *Trafalgar* and his war-time command, *James Cook*.

That had been a warship, pure and simple, the *James Cook*. Everything built during the war had been engineered with economy of space in mind. There had been no display cases nor much in the way of leg room. Before the war, things weren't much better. Clayton remembered the first few ships he'd served on making runs from Zoar to Selene and the outer posts of the system. Those trips reminded him of descriptions he'd read of early transoceanic sailing on Earth. Modern conditions were far more sanitary, of course, but the profession was still far from glamorous. The war had changed that.

Now the focus of the entire world was on the merging Exosphere and Next Frontier companies and glamour attended that. Director of the Fleet Thaddeus Bear held more power and influence than anyone since the last Captain of the Planet, almost a thousand years ago. It was no surprise that he spared no expense to keep his upper management happy. And Clayton was happy. Mostly. There was still that nagging distrust of Spadt. He needed to do something about it, but what? There was nothing he *could* do but watch and wait, and Clayton didn't like the idea of being on edge throughout this whole voyage.

With a sigh he leaned forward and pressed an icon on his desk. It chirped in response. "Message to Commander Spadt: his presence requested in the captain's cabin." The desk warbled an affirmative and Clayton sat back, rubbing his eyes. Information was always valuable. Maybe talking to Spadt would ease Clayton's apprehension. He opened a drawer in his desk and withdrew a dark bottle and two small glasses. When the door chimed, Clayton uncorked the bottle.

"Enter." Clayton looked up as the door slid open and his first officer, Commander Elias Spadt, ducked his head slightly entering through the low door. "Thank you for coming, commander." Clayton poured the two glasses, the liquid a thin, white-gold color. Clayton stopped the bottle and picked them up. He stepped around the desk, holding one out to Spadt. "I thought it would be appropriate to toast the beginning of our voyage."

Spadt accepted the drink with a nod. "Aye, captain." He raised the glass. "To *Trafalgar*." Clayton noted how quickly Spadt made the toast. Was it a play to ingratiate himself with Clayton? Perhaps it was genuine. Since meeting Spadt, Clayton had found him to be quick and decisive, always on top of things, never quite exceeding his authority. If he knew he could trust Spadt, Clayton wouldn't have any other kind of man as his second, but his observations so far did nothing to tell him whether or not Spadt was genuine.

"*Trafalgar*." Clayton touched his glass to Spadt's. "May she carry us the distance safely." He tipped back his drink and set the empty glass on the desk behind him. He sat down on the desk and regarded Spadt. "I remember when the *James Cook* launched, there was nothing. No ceremony. That wasn't how things used to be."

Spadt's brow furrowed. "For as long as I remember, there hasn't been much ceremony."

"True enough. Ever since humankind came to Zoar, at least. But back on Earth, there were traditions that went back centuries. Based on superstitions, most of them. Still, I think a little something to mark the occasion—even just a drink." Spadt nodded and stepped toward Clayton.

He held out his hand. "May I?"

Clayton followed the line of Spadt's arm to the whiskey bottle. "By all means." He handed it to Spadt, who poured two more shots, handing the second to Clayton.

"To new traditions."

"And new comrades." They drank.

There was silence for a moment, then Spadt said, "Captain, I get the impression you don't like me."

Clayton's eyes flicked to the side. "You've been a huge help ever since we were assigned to *Trafalgar*. I couldn't have asked for a better first officer."

Spadt inclined his head. "I've done my job, sir. That's not what I'm talking about. This is the first time you've spoken to me off duty. We've been serving together for almost a month."

Clayton twisted his empty glass in his hand. "I'd be lying if I said I've been dying to get to know you."

"Not a very straightforward answer."

Clayton met Spadt's eye. "I am the captain, commander. I don't have to explain myself to you, not on matters that are unimportant to the overall operation of the ship." He stood up and walked around the far side of his desk. He had not intended for the conversation to go this way. But now was not the time to soften. He sighed and lowered his shoulders.

"This voyage we're on ... it's unlike anything any living Renovaman has done before. At the same time, it's not so different from the voyages our ancestors took two or three millennia ago." He turned back to Spadt. "I studied that period of history, commander. What most people, including those aboard this ship don't realize is that without iron discipline, we won't finish the trip." He walked right up close to Spadt and forced eye contact again.

"What I need—what the ship needs—from you is not a friend. What I do need is for you to follow my orders and uphold the doctrine I put down on this ship. If the authority of the captain fails, this ship is dead in space. Is that understood?"

"Yes, sir."

"Good." Clayton nodded and stepped back from Spadt. "Now, as far as ship's operations go, do you have anything to report?"

"No, sir. Everything is on schedule and running smoothly."

"Glad to hear it." Clayton turned and looked at the *James Cook* in the display case.

"Captain, may I ask where we're going?"

Clayton took a deep breath. "I'm not at liberty to say until the admiral informs me."

"That hardly seems necessary."

"It's not up to me, commander." Clayton faced him again. "The fact of the matter is that certain details of our mission are so sensitive that the Admiralty has ordered complete secrecy for at least two weeks. Longer, if Admiral Villeneuve sees fit. As soon as I can, I will tell you. The secrecy is well justified." Clayton hesitated, almost adding that he didn't like to keep secrets, that he preferred to show trust in his officers. But he didn't and he knew why. Spadt caught his eye and stared him down. Clayton held his gaze for a moment, then decided he had to assert his authority again.

"In the event that I am incapacitated, control will transfer to you and my orders will be unsealed for you. Is that satisfactory, commander?"

"Sir, that's not what I—"

"Is that satisfactory?"

"Yes, sir."

Clayton held back a sigh. "Everything you need to know now, you know. Anything more you will need to know I'll tell you then. You're dismissed, commander." Spadt tilted his head and exited the room, again ducking under the doorframe. Once the door shut behind him, Clayton put his face in his hands and rubbed his eyes. That had backfired. Now Spadt likely trusted Clayton no more than Clayton trusted him, which was no way to run a ship. Clayton let out a sigh, then a yawn. A good night's sleep was what he needed. He checked the time on his desk—2017 Zoar time and no paperwork. Hell, he'd already had a nightcap of sorts; he'd work on the Spadt problem in the morning.

CHAPTER VI

The Chief sends me to the cave
To wait before the battle long
He knows its coming
He knows its marching in the night
On my way I feel the cold
'Jeli'ahsh oh Jeli'ahsh take my child
'Take his coming
Take his coming, rolling like the tide.'
—Traditional Meltesh Children's Song

Fred didn't know how long he'd been on the planet. Maybe it hadn't been all that long, but the days stretched on forever, and he had no idea how long he'd been out after the crash. For the time he had been conscious, he had counted three distinct days, providing he'd slept through the day of the crash, but he knew that days here were longer than they were back home. Dr. Murdock still lay in the other hammock. She hadn't so much as stirred the entire time. She wouldn't last much longer.

Fred tried to push those thoughts out of his mind. There was nothing he could do, even if he himself wasn't bedridden. Shar'hre checked on Dr. Murdock every time she came to feed Fred or take the bowl that served as a bedpan. She spoke to him, but Fred felt no desire to respond with anything more than singular words. He'd seen no one other than Shar'hre and the people who were there when he crawled out of the escape pod, though he imagined there must be a significant population around.

Who were they? Fred couldn't be sure, but he had nothing to do but guess as he sat in the hammock, watching Shar'hre as she wove some kind of flat, thin material into what he guessed would be a bowl. They had to be human; there was just too much that was similar for them not to be. But how had they ended up here? Earth's survivors lived on Zoar now. Why were there such distinct differences between these people and humans on Zoar, with their slitted pupils and skin that came in patches like a pinta horse's coat? Not to mention that if Shar'hre was a typical example of these people's size, they stood half a foot taller than the average human from Zoar. She looked stronger too, with clearly defined muscles and no fat to speak of.

He watched her, frowning, still trying to piece it all together when the sound of shouting reached Fred from outside. Shar'hre stood suddenly. She exited the hut without so much as a glance at him. He sat up, hands gripping the large frond-like leaves of the hammock beneath him. The voices grew louder for a few moments before quieting. Fred's grip on the leaves tightened.

She returned, a man with curly red hair and a beard close behind. The man stood several inches over Shar'hre and carried a clay bowl in both hands. The leaves that made up his attire were blue and light purple and a sword hung by his side. His skin bore similar patches to Shar'hre's. She stood to the side, watching as the man approached Fred. Fred straightened up, pushing himself back in the hammock.

The man came closer and shifted the bowl into one hand. With the other, he dipped two fingers into the bowl. As he sat down on the edge of the hammock, he reached out with them towards Fred's face. Fred could see light shining on the man's wet fingers and he turned to one side as a pungently sweet, vinegary smell assaulted his nose. The man smeared the substance on the bridge of Fred's nose. Fred coughed and squirmed, but the man continued to rub the paste into his skin. As he breathed in the fumes, Fred began to feel lightheaded.

The man began to speak, but Fred only heard a vague buzzing as he struggled to breath past the smell. The man reached his fingers back into the bowl, repeating his earlier process. Fred tried to turn away again, but his eyelids grew heavy. The last thing he saw was the black, slit pupils in the man's eyes.

Hrintar finished the blessing and moved from Hred's hammock across to Dor'othee. Her breathing had become yet more shallow. Shar'hre had changed her dressing not long before, for what little good it did. She was glad Hrintar had come. As he began the prayer, Shar'hre looked away and found her eyes upon Hred. He was unconscious, as was to be expected after a *hroulnun* blessing. At least, that was what she'd been told. Until now, Shar'hre had observed only Hrintar's *hroulnun* after he returned from his *shremen* beyond the Five Brothers. It was strange to think that it was only three cycles of the Greater Moon past that he began to preach and prophesy of the arrival of Telahren. Shar'hre wondered if he had known just how soon they would arrive.

Hrintar finished the blessing and stood. Shar'hre straightened unconsciously as he approached her. One of his lieutenants came and took the bowl of *linhru'in* from him and he put a hand on Shar'hre's shoulder.

"How long does she have?"

Shar'hre sighed. "I expect she will be gone by the end of the day."

Hrintar nodded. "I will return in the morning and we will perform her *dunul*. For now, I must return to Gid'Del. Genit and Ema'eln press me still." He took his hand off her shoulder and looked back at Fred. "Will he be able to travel soon?"

Shar'hre frowned at Hrintar. "I don't know. His leg is healing but the pain is still great. How far?"

"Only to Gid'Del. I wish to present him to the Keem."

Shar'hre sighed. "A few days, at least. I will try to get him on his feet when he awakens."

"Good." Hrintar moved in front of Shar'hre and held her shoulders in his hands. "I must leave now, love." He placed a kiss on her forehead. "*Ipsun*," he murmured as he pulled away.

"Ipsun." Shar'hre rubbed his arm gently and he smiled slightly before sliding past her and out the door.

Fred could hear a breeze blowing past the hut as he limped around it, arm wrapped around Shar'hre's waist. It had taken her pulling him out of the hammock for Fred to comprehend that she wanted to try and get him walking. He couldn't have made it far without Shar'hre's assistance, but it was a relief to get out of the hammock. Every other step he took was laborious and careful. Too much weight on his bad leg and Fred knew he'd drop right to the ground.

Shar'hre spoke and guided Fred towards the doorway, then out into the open air. He held up his free arm to block the sunlight. Once his eyes adjusted to the brightness, his jaw dropped. Immediately in front of him a wide dirt path extended both left and right. The grass on its edges was a mixture of vibrant greens and pale reds and oranges.

Beyond the path, a forest extended down a gentle slope. Most of the forest was different shades of green but there were patches that were light blue, while others were yellow. The trunks that weren't obscured by long, drooping leaves were white with black speckles, not unlike Earth's birch trees, but the similarities ended there. To Fred, they looked like someone had softened spaghetti noodles then froze them in place. In the distance, a mountain range extended away from the forest.

A peal of laughter from over his right ear brought him out of his reverie. He looked over to see a look of mirth on Shar'hre's face as she continued to laugh. Only then did Fred realize his mouth had been open.

"It's ... beautiful."

Shar'hre's laughter stopped as she looked at him with a furrowed brow, "Bew-dih-ful?"

Fred gestured to the landscape with his free arm, "This place: it's amazing." It gave his childhood home in the woods of Tamarack a run for its money, but Fred had always felt drawn to pictures of the more tropical places of Zoar, places like Palm City. The trees there, with leaves similar to these forests of Geneva, had been their greatest allure.

Shar'hre nodded and said something that sounded like trees. Fred looked at her, wondering if the word was indeed related. If the people here had come from Earth, the connection would make sense. The English of the Renovamen had descended from American English and this word similarity was one of a number Fred had picked out that reminded him of a number of linguistic classrooms at Greenacre University Sequoia. His focus had been on Castellano Spanish, which, despite being twelve hundred years dead, still bore a number of cognates to modern Renovamen English.

Shar'hre sighed contentedly, bringing his attention back to the view. Several small, triangular shapes dotted the sky, drifting like clouds. Some kind of airborne creature? Fred glanced back at the forest just as a warm wind came up from behind them and gusted gently through the trees. A shimmering blue wave traveled down the slope as the leaves of the trees were blown upward. Fred gasped and his eyes widened. It was like ocean waves or fields of grain back home, but so much more vibrant. He stared for a moment, then looked at Shar'hre. She smiled at him. Her eyes had slowly but steadily melted the past few days. Where once he'd seen ice, now he saw a summer sky.

"I know you probably don't understand me, but ... thanks. I really appreciate everything you've done for me." Shar'hre continued to smile as Fred's thoughts turned to Dr. Murdock back in the hut. He swallowed a rising lump in his throat. He hadn't gotten to know her very well. In all honesty, he hadn't gone to any effort to get to know anyone on the crew. He wondered if... No. Fred shook his head. Best not to get his hopes up. Shar'hre cleared her throat. Fred snapped his look over to her and she gestured toward the path.

Fred nodded. "Yeah, let's walk."

With Shar'hre's help, Fred limped onto the path. They turned right and Fred was presented with a view that could have come from any number of places on the outskirts of Sequoia. The dirt path disappeared into the distance, flanked on either side by rustling leaves. It was nostalgic and, for a moment, Fred felt homesick.

Then pain flared through his leg and he stumbled. His arm slipped from around Shar'hre and he braced himself for a rough landing. It never came. Shar'hre's arm was still around him, holding him up around his armpits. She smiled as if he were no heavier than a feather.

"Dammit!" Fred sagged, making no attempt to stand again, "Put me down!" A look of concern and confusion crossed Shar'hre's face. "Put me down, dammit!" Hesitantly she lowered Fred to the ground where he sat, legs out in front of him. He pulled his hands through his hair, inhaling quickly. Shar'hre sat down a few feet away from him, staring at Fred.

"What're you looking at?" Color flushed Fred's face and he stared at the ground between them. Shar'hre said nothing. They sat in silence for a few moments.

Then Shar'hre stood up and extended a hand. "Gumun." Fred looked at her hand for a moment before returning his gaze to the dirt.

"Gumun!" Shar'hre repeated. When Fred still didn't take her hand, Shar'hre bent down and hauled him into a standing position, grumbling. With her arm once again wrapped around him, Shar'hre started back to the hut quickly, practically dragging Fred along. The sudden movement and fast pace caught Fred off guard and he hopped on his good leg to keep up. In a matter of moments Shar'hre was brushing aside the massive yellow leaves that covered the doorway and they were in the hut, where she unceremoniously dropped Fred on his hammock.

When Shar'hre spoke again her voice softened, but still bit into him. With a few unintelligible sentences, Shar'hre turned and left the hut. Fred looked up at the ceiling and brought an open palm down on his leg. He groaned in pain and twisted onto his side. Across the room he saw Murdock lying in her hammock, as still as ever.

"Get it together, Fred."

Shar'hre awoke before the sun rose. She quickly grew alertness and swung her legs over the side of the hammock, making immediately for Dor'othee. She lifted the wrist to check for a pulse but there was no need; her hand was cold. The Telahren had been dead for several hours. Shar'hre looked down at the woman and sighed.

"At peace, Messenger. At peace." She laid Dor'othee's hand on her chest and turned to look at Hred. His chest rose and fell steadily. Shar'hre shook her head and stepped out of the mah. The Lesser Moon sat on the tree line, its light turning the tops of the leaves white. Shar'hre lowered herself to sit against the doorway and looked up into the sky. Despite the brightness, it was still possible to pick out a few of the brighter stars. Most of the Telahren was still visible, but the two mountains of Hranhro's Constellation were washed out.

Shar'hre closed her eyes and let out a long breath. She had not failed. As much as she felt each life she helped, she felt each death. For Dor'othee there was nothing more she could have done; the Telahren had been doomed to death long before Shar'hre even heard of her Descent. And Hred was still alive. Shar'hre still felt sorrow, however, just as she had with each *dehihrah* who died under her care: Gohruthin who had died in her arms a few months past; Lu'in's stillborn child; and Hahlia when Shar'hre had first set out on her own as *no'ihrah*. With each, Shar'hre learned more about death. She did not fear it; she never had.

Each had their time, and the pain Gohruthin and Dor'othee had felt made their deaths a release in the end, just as Hahlia's life of experience made her passing right in the world. Knowing that did not make the experience easier. The knowledge that they had moved on, that they were reunited with the Jeli'ahsh did. As her *di'er* had told her many times before she left, it was that emotion for others and that faith that made Shar'hre a good no'ihrah.

Shar'hre looked up into the sky. The moon was below the tree line now and the stars shone brighter. A few wins floated above in the near dark, and she smiled at their serene passage. They were gone from view moments later. She lingered a while before returning to the mah. She had to prepare for the dunul.

When Fred woke up neither Shar'hre nor Dr. Murdock were in the hut. It didn't take long for Fred to determine that Murdock had died. He lay back in his cot and swallowed as he closed his eyes. That made it official—he was the only one left. He found himself gripping the edge of the hammock and forced himself to let go and realized he was holding his breath as well. He let it go too. There was nothing for it. If it weren't for Shar'hre and the rest of her people, he wouldn't have survived either. He was lucky.

He scoffed and grimaced. In a way, this was exactly what he'd wanted when he left Zoar. He was finally free of everything that place represented. Free of civil strife and corporate capitalism, free of another war, of the fear of the next building over collapsing in the middle of the night. And what had it cost? Not much: just the lives of eighteen people and the hope of speaking to his friends and family again. Fred sighed and turned in the hammock which set it swinging more than he'd meant to.

As he tried to steady it without falling out, he saw Shar'hre come in through the door. Distracted by her sudden appearance, he tipped over and the hammock swung out from under him. He smacked into the ground with a thud. He heard her laugh as a dull ache spread through his body.

He propped himself up on an arm. "Gee, thanks."

Shar'hre spoke as she approached him. He couldn't understand what she said but her voice quickly turned from a playful lilt to a somber tone. She held her hand out to him and he took it. She pulled him up and put her arm around his shoulder. Somewhat hesitantly, Fred put his arm around her waist, and they moved toward the door. He felt a little more up to walking than he had the day before, but he wondered what was going on outside.

He didn't have to wonder long. Just down the path from the hut a body lay on a raised platform: Dorothy's body. As they approached and Fred saw more, he realized that the platform was a pyre. Apparently, these people practiced cremation. Several people, all taller than him, stood around the pyre, including the redhead who had smeared that foul-smelling stuff on Fred's face the day before.

They came to a stop directly in front of the pyre. Fred looked down at Dorothy's body and found that he couldn't get a deep breath. Though one side of her face was red from the burns, she looked peaceful. She was still covered in purple leaves, but these looked fresher than those she'd had on before.

Fred shook his head. "I'm sorry, doctor. Dorothy," he whispered.

The redhead spoke and Fred looked over at him. He seemed to be addressing the group. His voice was calming. Fred listened, trying to focus and pull apart some of the words, but the redhead kept it brief. He turned and looked at Fred. Fred wasn't sure what he expected, but everyone was looking at him, so he cleared his throat. Maybe they wanted a eulogy or something. It occurred to Fred that he could say anything at all, and they wouldn't understand. He suppressed a sardonic chuckle and forced a deep breath. He looked at Dorothy.

"I hardly knew you, doctor. To be entirely honest, you struck me as being pretty arrogant. I remember that you didn't usually eat your dessert packets, but you gave them to Dr. Shin or Lieutenant Haystrom instead of just throwing them in the disposal. You were thoughtful about those kinds of things. You always reset your chair when you were done, which I appreciated. Nothing bothered me more on that ship than tripping over everyone's chairs when I made rounds."

Fred paused and swallowed. "Rest in peace, Dorothy." He looked down at his feet and back up. The redhead watched him intently, nodding. Fred gave him a short nod. He felt Shar'hre pulling him away from the pyre and moved with her, stepping gingerly on his bad leg. Once they were away from the pyre, the redhead moved in front of the it, holding something in both hands. He scraped the two things together over the pyre and Fred saw sparks. After a few more scrapes, the pyre caught, and the redhead retreated. It wasn't long until the pyre was burning steadily. The redhead stepped up to the pyre and added a branch.

He stepped back and looked towards Fred and Shar'hre. Another man approached and handed them each a branch. They moved back towards the pyre. Fred couldn't bring himself to look directly at Dorothy as the heat assailed him and tossed his stick into the flame a moment after Shar'hre. They stepped back and watched as the rest of the group stepped forward and added their own branches.

They stood and watched the pyre burn. No more fuel was added. The others filtered off, walking down the road, away from the hut and pyre. Eventually only the redhead remained with Shar'hre and Fred. After a while, he approached them. He nodded to Fred, nearly bowing. Fred returned the nod and the redhead turned to Shar'hre and spoke gently. She responded in a quiet voice. The redhead took her head in his hands and placed a kiss on her forehead. Then he nodded to her and moved past them, following the others away from the pyre.

The day passed slowly, as was typical of a dunul. With insufficient mourners, it was Shar'hre's responsibility as no'ihrah to see the pyre burned to the ground and did not spread. Hred seemed content to sit and watch it burn. It was not uncommon for those closest to the dead to remain for a time and it was not all that different from what Hred had spent the past few days doing. Shar'hre wondered at him, as she often did. Hrintar said that the arrival of the Messengers *was* the message. Even before Hred and Dor'othee had come, he had taught that the Jeli'ahsh would not need their voices. But how were the Meltesh to know how to prepare to be re-united with the Jeli'ahsh if the Telahren did not guide them? She did not doubt the Tuluchur; all would come in its own time. She simply did not see the path forward, regardless of how much she pondered on it.

Hred offered no clues. She looked to him as she exited the mah with a jug of water and a bowl of dried *ladra.* He sat with his back against a tree, one knee up, his injured leg stretched out before him. He stared into the smoldering pyre until she drew near him. She took a swallow of water from the jug and offered it to him. He took it with a word. As he drank, she lowered herself onto the ground next to him. She picked out a piece of ladra and tore it in half. She held half to Hred who took it with another murmur. They both looked out at the pyre and Shar'hre chewed on the ladra slowly, savoring the sweet coating as it mixed with the bitter fruit. All was quiet except for the crackling of the fire and buzzing of the forest. Shar'hre finished her ladra and offered Hred another piece. He took it and they continued to eat in silence.

Hred broke the silence. Shar'hre looked at him. He scoffed and looked down, back at the pyre. He continued to speak. Shar'hre thought his voice sounded almost sarcastic: softer than usual and slightly more nasal. But it was earnest too, even when he chuckled and shook his head. Whatever he was saying, he meant it. She wondered what he might be saying. It was the most he had spoken since his arrival. She imagined he was reflecting on Dor'othee, maybe thinking about the Jeli'ahsh or whatever it was he was sup-posed to do now.

He stopped and took hold of the jug, swigging from it. Then he continued, his voice lighter, amused but still with that ironic edge. He stopped and sighed, letting his good leg drop alongside the other. He picked up a pebble and threw it to the side of the pyre.

After a moment's pause, Shar'hre put a hand on his shoulder. "All is well," she said. "She has returned to the Jeli'ahsh." Hred looked at her and gave her a half smile and she wondered if all really was well. She supposed even the Telahren were subject to grief. As it was taught, the Jeli'ahsh were relatives of the Meltesh and the other peoples of Galjirn. Their elevated stature did not mean they were immune to all the weaknesses by which the Meltesh were afflicted. Yet it made her wonder: just how mortal and fallible were the Jeli'ahsh?

CHAPTER VII

After all, such a total and catastrophic departure from not just a homeland but a home world, demanded reexamination of ancient teachings, regardless of one's faith. Indeed, it may well be why there are so few atheists recorded among the people born in exile.
—From "Why Now?" by Tobin Gorokhov

The marines ran laps around the ship as they had every day since coming aboard a week before. Following these five miles would be a workout led by Sergeant Major Fegan. The oval shape of the corridors on the middle decks made them ideal for PT; once around was almost precisely one mile. The changes in scenery were negligible, but it was easier on their knees than stopping and turning around every time they reached the end of a half mile or pounding endlessly on the treadmill.

It also allowed Kobayashi to observe her troops in an organic way, watching as groups came into shape, based mostly on ability. The old corporate war divisions were pale, faded in this platoon. Goldman was possibly the fittest marine she had. He consistently ran with the front pack and gave no ground in other areas of PT, even when matched against Mithril. Given their status as Special Operations, she suspected they would leave him behind if they could. Fegan also ran as part of that front group, while Holtz was in the next group back. Johansen ran ahead of Kobayashi, typically caught between groups. Kobayashi herself kept pace with Allred, solidly in the middle margin, though she expected that some of the men who ran behind her could outrun her without much effort. Given the purpose of these runs, however, there was no need to crack the whip.

At the beginning of the fourth lap, Allred spoke, as she often did. "I miss running on solid ground. The sun beating down, maybe a bit of a breeze. Scenery."

"Yeah," Kobayashi said.

"I actually started to like running when I was at the Academy. The campus was beautiful."

"I've only been there once. It was nice."

"Right." Allred trailed off. After a moment she said, "What was it like for you? Training, I mean. During the war."

"Nonexistent."

"What?

"There was no training. At least, until things went to hell there wasn't. Then security gave everyone a crash course and asked for volunteers."

"And you were one of them?"

Kobayashi shook her head. "No."

"What do you mean?" Allred's voice rose. "I didn't think there was a draft or anything like that."

"There wasn't. I just did what I had to."

"Oh." Silence fell again and went uninterrupted for most of a mile. "How did you end up as an officer?"

"Everyone needs a job."

The remainder of the run passed in silence. As each group finished, the platoon mustered outside the cargo bay that served as their gym. While there were fitness facilities aboard, the setup of machines and weights was not conducive to group drills or sparring. Additionally, those facilities were limited; taking the entire platoon in would leave no room for the ship's crew.

The whole platoon assembled in a grid, except Fegan and Kobayashi. Fegan then put them through a number of exercises and stretches and divided them into groups of five to spar. The groups were independent of squad divisions and were never the same day to day, though most of the time there was some rough correlation in skill. Today, however, Kobayashi noted that there was more disparity this time. Allred and another greenhorn were in a group with Johansen and a couple members of Mithril. Fegan had put Kobayashi in with Goldman and a few of the other newly enlisted. Fegan was not the only qualified instructor, but it was his turn to coach the session.

The matches followed a simple structure: two people fought until one subdued the other. Limited strikes were allowed and no holds were barred, but there was a limit on the amount of punishment one could put out. While they waited until after the run and calisthenics in order to cut down on injuries, it remained the responsibility of the other three in any group to ensure that no one went too far.

Today, that didn't matter. While Kobayashi observed the first match in her group, she heard an unusually loud smack. She looked over to the next group and saw Johansen standing over an opponent. Whoever it was twisted on the ground, hands to their face. Fegan rushed over and crouched over the injured person. After a moment, he helped her to her feet and Kobayashi saw that it was Allred. He made eye contact with Kobayashi.

"Broken nose," he said. "I'll get her to medical."

"I'll take over."

"Thank you, major."

Kobayashi nodded and stepped out of her circle. She approached Johansen's group and motioned to two of the other marines. "Looks like Captain Johansen won that bout. Next pair, keep it clean."

"Yes, ma'am." They circled each other and Kobayashi stayed for a moment, but her eyes were on Johansen, who watched the match intently. Kobayashi moved on to the next group.

Fegan returned with Allred fifteen minutes or so after taking her to medical and the two had joined Kobayashi on her rounds. Now, as the platoon filtered out of the cargo bay, Kobayashi headed Johansen off.

"Captain Johansen, I'd like a word." Johansen stopped a few feet from the door, a gym bag over her shoulder. She turned to face Kobayashi. The air was quiet, heavy with the heat and sweat that remained from sparring men and women. Johansen's face was devoid of emotion, but her body was stiff, arms crossed, betraying her annoyance.

"Yes, major?"

"We can talk and walk." Kobayashi gestured to the door. "Has your team been outfitted yet?" They walked together out into the hall.

"Not yet. Now that fabrication is complete, my team's slotted for calibration tests tomorrow."

"I'd like to be there, if you don't mind."

"It's not going to be anything exciting."

"Still, I'd like to be there."

Johansen shrugged. "Suit yourself, major." Johansen glanced down, then pulled a hand through her hair, clearing her throat. "Is there anything else?"

"I was wondering if you'd like to have breakfast with me."

"What, are you trying to buddy up with me?"

"A certain familiarity with one's subordinates is essential to a cohesive unit."

Johansen attempted to restrain a hard exhalation, but Kobayashi heard it. "Permission to speak freely, ma'am?"

"Go ahead."

"You sound like a real cold bitch."

Kobayashi's cheeks flushed. "You're not the first to tell me that. Is that going to be a problem?"

"Hell no, major. I'm a cold bitch too."

The first week sailing had gone smoothly. Clayton sat behind his desk going through the reports from all departments. Nothing seemed wrong, though a few department heads, including Major Kobayashi, had reported concerns about morale. Clayton had expected that. The secret nature of their mission might have been exciting if the crew weren't wary of crewmates who had fought on opposite sides of the war. As it was, Clayton suspected that it was more cause for suspicion among the crew; even if everyone truly bought into integration, there had to be some lingering distrust. His own interactions with Commander Spadt proved that.

Clayton checked the time: 1126 Zoar time. He was due to meet with Villeneuve and Captain Amin shortly. He grimaced. He didn't much care for Villenueve; the man's service record was almost completely blank. Most of the Admiralty had seen little to no action during the war. They had been the ones calling the shots, rarely in danger, rarely exposed to the horror of war. Most of the responsible parties for the war had been ousted during Director Bear's peace negotiation or purged when he took the Directorship, but Clayton doubted that there weren't still a number of highly placed officers still around who'd had their hands in the start of the war. Regardless of whether or not Villeneuve was one of those, Clayton did not trust him to be an effective tactician. He'd done nothing to earn his position as a military leader.

Captain Amin on the other hand... Clayton had only met her briefly before departure, but he had studied her file carefully. She was a clever one. A Next Frontier officer, she'd risen to the rank of captain shortly after Clayton and proven to be a formidable opponent. He had never fought her, but her war record told him a great deal. Across fifteen engagements, both solo and in formations, she had disabled six ships and captured seven. Clayton himself had disabled seven and captured nine over the course of seventeen. It was no surprise that the NF half of the Admiralty had chosen her to captain the other Nelson-class.

He checked the clock on his desk display again: 1129. Time for the meeting. Clayton, stood and walked around to the open space of the office. He reached back and tapped a blinking icon on his desk. The overhead lights dimmed slightly. Two purple lights swept the room, one vertically, the other horizontally. Clayton clasped his hands behind his back. A moment passed and two people appeared in the room, their holographic images slightly clipped. Amin was to Clayton's right. Villeneuve stood in front of both of them.

"Captain Clayton. Captain Amin. I hope things are going well thus far." Villeneuve looked from one to the other.

Amin gave a ready salute. "No issues to report, but it's early yet, admiral."

"Likewise, sir." Clayton offered his own salute.

Villeneuve turned and took a couple steps away from Clayton and Amin. He clasped his hands behind his back and turned to face them. "I imagine you're wondering why we're having this meeting." Clayton inclined his head. There was no obvious reason to have a meeting like this, across ships while traveling faster than light, instead of simply submitting status reports. There had to be more to the briefing they'd been given prior to departure.

"Well, here's the gist of it. Preliminary data from *Erikson* suggested that there's intelligent life on Geneva. Joint Command didn't want this information going public until they knew for sure what they were going to do about it, so I was under orders to wait until we were well away before disseminating the information."

Clayton's shoulders tensed and he did his best to slow his breathing and relax them imperceptibly. Intelligent alien life. It was a given, considering the Presidents fate, but were those responsible also the inhabitants of Geneva? If so, why the long wait before attacking *Erikson*? If the sentient life on Geneva was independent from those who kidnapped the Presidents, there was no telling how they might react to humanity's existence, or even how humanity would react to theirs.

Amin interrupted his thoughts. "What evidence?" A good question. Clayton looked from her to Villeneuve.

"Photographs across several land masses showed signs of irregular interruptions in the environment. Grey spots in the middle of fields, large swaths of scorched land and the like. Nothing definitive." Villeneuve waved a hand dismissively. "It's probably nothing. Nevertheless, it would be prudent not to inform your crews. The longer we can keep this information from leaking out, the better." Clayton furrowed his brow and nodded, but refrained from saying anything. That wasn't definitive. So why bother bringing it up at all? Glancing sideways, he thought he saw Amin pulling her lower lip in slightly before speaking.

"Aye, sir. We'll keep it on the downlow." Clayton nodded, allowing Amin's answer to serve for him as well. He didn't agree with Villeneuve's sentiment, and he doubted that it would take long for one of the doys in his or Amin's science department to see what *Erikson* had and figure something was up. Clayton didn't trust the Admiralty to make the correct conclusion if the planet proved to already be inhabited. And, now that he was thinking about it, *Erikson* was a Darwin-class science ship. Even with data compression, it would have been able to send back more than just vague pictures of the planet's surface.

"Alright then," Villeneuve said, "the next item of business is to establish our strategy upon arrival. Thoughts, Captain Amin?"

"Yes, sir. Now, given that we don't know anything about the enemy that destroyed *Erikson*, we'll need to ensure that we have positional advantage." At this, Amin's fingers flew over an invisible desk and a holographic image of three spheres, one large, the others smaller, appeared between the three officers. "Geneva has two moons, orbiting on the same plane. I propose that the *Nile* take up a position in orbit of the outer moon while the *Tovey* and *Trafalgar* orbit Geneva. That should allow us to keep an eye on each other, the planet, and external space easily and with minimal power usage. And we can begin searching for Geneva for survivors. This is, of course, providing the alien craft isn't waiting for us when we arrive." Clayton nodded, his chin resting in his hand as he studied the schematic. It made sense.

"Your thoughts, captain?"

Clayton inclined his head to Amin. "A good plan. As far as entering the system goes, I suggest a staggered arrival. *Trafalgar* will enter the system first. Five minutes later, *Nile* and *Tovey* fifteen minutes after that."

"Smart." Amin was nodding. "*Trafalgar* gets an eye on the situation. If she needs reinforcements immediately, I'll be there. Delaying *Tovey*'s arrival can turn the element of surprise in our favor." She looked at Clayton with the left side of her mouth twitching upward. "Providing we hold out for that long."

Clayton returned the smirk. "I think that between the two of us, we'll be fine." He was beginning to like Amin.

"And after we jump in? What's the plan then, Clayton?"

Clayton looked at Villeneuve, somewhat surprised. "Sir, we don't know the first thing about the enemy's armament and while we only expect one ship, there could be more by the time we arrive. If a battle ensues, we've got the combined Exo and NF playbook, but ultimately, we're going to be playing this by ear."

Villeneuve frowned. "I don't like the idea of going into this unprepared. I want both of you to work on battle plans." Clayton dropped his gaze for a second, bringing it back up when Amin began speaking.

"Of course, sir," Amin gave Villeneuve a short nod, "but Captain Clayton has a point. It pays to be flexible in unknown situations."

Clayton nodded in assent. "Given our experience, I suggest Captain Amin or myself direct strategy in battle. But you're right, admiral, we should have some options prepared before we arrive." There had rarely been opportunities for Clayton to gather his thoughts during the war, let alone plan elaborate strategies but for once, he had the time and the opportunity to truly prepare. He should have thought to come to the briefing with more than thoughts on who should arrive first.

"See to it then, captain. Villeneuve out." He held his hand out, pressing an invisible button and faded away. Clayton was surprised at Villeneuve's abrupt departure. Most of his superiors during the war always ensured there was an opportunity for their officers to bring their own concerns to their attention.

"Well, that was enlightening." Amin was looking at him, arms crossed. Clayton was surprised she hadn't cut her own connection after Villeneuve had.

Clayton sat down on the edge of his desk, holding his legs out in front of him. "You can tell he spent the war behind a desk. Thanks for backing me up there."

Amin smiled and shrugged, strolling a few feet to Clayton's right. "You know how it is. No plan survives contact with the enemy. Doesn't make sense to develop in depth strategies that go right out the window once your opponent deviates from the script. Good touch, having *Tovey* jump in last."

Clayton crossed his arms. "I expected a little more hostility from N.F.'s most effective commander."

"I could say the same about Exo's most effective captain." Amin chuckled. "I've spent the last couple years forcing myself to bring my emotions in line with the reality of the Joint Fleet." She paused, and Clayton could tell that she was looking out the small viewport behind the desk in her office, which was identical to his. "And I have a great deal of respect for you, captain."

"Likewise, captain. Your record is impressive to say the least, and you seem to be living up to it in person. I'm glad we never met in battle."

"Oh? You don't think you could beat me?" She looked back at him, smirking.

"Maybe. Maybe not. I'd rather not find out. I'm not one to play with my crew's lives." Clayton stood and uncrossed his arms, going to look out at the void through his own porthole.

"Neither am I, captain. But surely you're curious."

"You know what they say. Curiosity killed the cat." Clayton looked back at Amin who watched him with crossed arms, the fingers of her right arm tapping her bicep in a repeating sequence, pinky up to forefinger.

"And satisfaction brought it back. How about a game of chess?"

A grin broke out on Clayton's face. "Alright, you're on. We've got plenty of downtime until we reach the Schweiz System anyway. I'm sure there's a chess program somewhere in the database."

Amin grinned back at him. "No need. I made sure to install my own on *Nile*. It'll just be a matter of sending it your way. I'll call you back this time tomorrow." She leaned down on the desk.

Clayton inclined his head. "Tomorrow then. Goodbye, captain."

"Goodbye."

Kobayashi watched Johansen pull the suit of armor up over her torso like a pair of coveralls. It was all white, though the black undersuit showed through gaps between the tiny microplates as they flexed at the joints and stretched before the suit settled around the woman's body. Large armor plates covered every place on Johansen's body where they wouldn't impede flexibility. The technician who had coached Johansen and Kobayashi through the basics of the suit when they first arrived approached, a tactile and a measuring tape in hand.

"Make a fist," he ordered. Johansen complied and the technician proceeded to measure every possible aspect of her arm, from the circumference of her fist to the distance between her splayed fingers. "Good, now release. Are you feeling any discomfort?" Johansen shook her head, and the technician nodded. "Now the other side." They repeated the process, then moved on to the rest of her body, taking every possible measurement. The technician had Johansen make all sorts of poses, flexes and stretches, even handing her a four-foot pole at one point. Kobayashi estimated it took a full fifteen minutes, maybe more.

When the technician finally stepped back, he nodded. "Alright, the fit looks good. Now, your helmet." He indicated the white, egg-like object that sat on a raised cart beside Johansen. Johansen picked it up. Attached at the bottom was a short, rubbery flap that ran around the entire lip of the helmet. She pulled it over her head and the flaps hung loosely over the high collar of the suit. She was faceless; only four small black dots marked the front of the helmet. Kobayashi didn't much care for the look.

"Now, ytuck that flap in all around; the material will pull together with the rest of your suit and create an airtight seal. Press your hand against your neck." Johansen did so and the technician nodded. "Good. Did anything feel irregular? Any bumps or bubbles?"

"No."

"Good. Now, I'm going to hook into your suit and initialize your software and diagnostic systems." The technician attached a cable to the base of Johansen's helmet and looked down at his tactile. "And 2... 1..." He was still looking down at his tactile. "Your heads-up display should be active now."

"It is."

"Good." The technician paused for a moment then nodded and looked up. "Diagnostics look good. You should have access to VATAS voice commands. You can also raise the face shield manually, if you press it in and slide it up." Johansen made no move to do so. "Would you mind doing that now to confirm there's no mechanical issue?" Johansen tilted her head to the side but complied. Underneath the mask was an opaque gold visor, reminiscent of those iconic helmets of Earth's early astronauts.

"Your cameras are pretty tough and will provide you with all the visual data you need, but in case they're damaged, and you need to raise the faceplate, keep in mind that that visor isn't rated for much in the way of blunt force or lasers. In other words, just because you've got a helmet on, don't go letting people hit you in the face. Aside from that concern, your most vulnerable point is going to be below your chin. The mechanics of getting that airtight seal required that no microplating go there. Any questions so far?"

"No."

"Alright, now we can run through the VATAS."

"No."

Kobayashi raised an eyebrow. Her surprise was shared by the technician.

"What?"

Kobayashi could see Johansen's sigh, though she didn't hear it.

"I think I can figure that out on my own."

"Listen, captain, there are a lot of aspects that go into the Visual and Aural Tact—"

"I can figure it out. Why are we wasting our time with this?"

Kobayashi stepped forward and crossed her arms. "Stand down, captain." The gold visor turned to look at Kobayashi. "This man's the expert and I expect you to listen to him. The last thing I need is a tactical blunder in the middle of an engagement because you don't understand the system you're working with."

"Yes, ma'am." Johansen did not move. Maybe it was just the armor that made her bearing seem stiff, but Kobayashi wondered about her initial refusal. For as removed from most of the platoon as Johansen seemed to be, Kobayashi had not noted her to be careless or incompetent.

"Alright, captain. Now the first thing you need to know about the VATAS is that it is only a supplement to your own situational awareness. Do not rely solely on it."

"Never intended to."

The technician folded his arms. "Right. Now, I'm sure you've noticed your rearview display in your HUD." Johansen nodded. "That's operated by two cameras in the back. They're the same grade as those on your front face plate. VATAS will also highlight moving figures. Anyone with a FID tag will be highlighted in green. Others will be in purple. You can alter those to fit your preference or environment. These suits are networked; VATAS can be ordered with voice commands to open channels with your unit as a whole or as individuals as well as other forces. You can also use the system to mark structures and objects, filter or isolate noise, capture audio and pictures and enhance both, in addition to thermal and night vision settings."

"What, am I going to be filming movies on this thing?"

"Mock it if you want, but being able to observe and record from a distance has a lot of tactical and strategic potential." The technician's eyebrows were drawn together in clear annoyance, but with a slight shake of his head, he continued his overview. "There's also radar and rangefinding features, like those standard to most tactical suites, as well as a chameleon unit integrated in the suit. It's not going to make you invisible, but it'll work in any environment from far enough away."

"Understood."

"I'd ask if you have any questions, but I think I know the answer to that. So instead, I'm just going to ask you to familiarize yourself with the functions and incorporate them into drills with your team." The technician looked at Kobayashi, who nodded. Then he turned back to Johansen. "You're free to go, captain." Johansen pulled the helmet off her head and took a sharp breath. She made eye contact briefly with Kobayashi, nodded and turned to leave.

"She's a peach, isn't she?"

Kobayashi watched Johansen go. "What would it take for me to get a suit like that?"

The technician shrugged. "We've got plenty of materials. Ask Captain Clayton. In my opinion, all you marines should be wearing something like this. Pretty damn reckless of the General Board and the Department of Innovation to have all you marines running around with nothing but a helmet and fatigues. But, I guess if most of you are like Captain Peach—"

"We're not." Kobayashi said. "You can be sure of that."

All was quiet on the bridge. Clayton lounged in his chair which sat in the center of the room. The floor was the same sterile white as the left side wall, that white that the bigshots and engineers at Integrated Command were enamored with. The rest of the bridge, however, was formed by a transparent bubble which was in turn wrapped in an armored shell with an array of cameras that gave a seamless and instantaneous feed from the outside. For now, the cameras were switched off, since the sight of an FTL corridor was enough to make even the hardiest of sailors sick after prolonged exposure.

Well below the captain's chair were a pair of seats with the same view, although the floor beneath them was transparent as well. Clayton's chief flight officer, Lieutenant Castaño, sat in the right seat tapping at his console as he prepared to initiate *Trafalgar's* exit. To Castaño's left was the ship's operations station from which ship systems could be monitored, ready to advise the captain and Castaño if something was amiss. On a level between them and Clayton were two platforms that stood six feet from the captain's chair. On the right was a tactical station, on the left the mission station. They were usually occupied by a tactical officer and either the executive officer or someone with pertinent expertise for the situation at hand. They were empty now, as were the auxiliary mission pods behind Clayton that could be manned by as many as ten crewmembers from various disciplines for additional analysis of everything from navigation and spectral analysis to geologic and atmospheric analysis.

Clayton shifted in his seat. There had been no opportunity to exercise those instruments since *Trafalgar's* commissioning. During a cruise like this, there was no need to have a full staff most of the time; it was just Clayton and Castaño holding down the fort for now. Clayton didn't much care for the design of the bridge. Being elevated above his subordinates helped in managing the bridge as a whole, but symbolically it proved problematic, given that his feet were at head level with anyone on the first level down from him, almost twice that for where Castaño sat now.

Clayton stood and descended the steps to Castaño's level, seating himself at the operations console. "All's well down here, lieutenant?"

"Aye, sir." Castaño swiveled his seat to face Clayton. "Very quiet. Deflection shields operating at stable capacity."

Clayton nodded. "Good. And how about you? Are you enjoying this assignment?"

Castaño bobbed his head. "It's good. Not much going on now, but I knew to expect that. This is exactly the kind of assignment I wanted. This is what I wanted to be doing before … everything."

"Me too. I knew Exosphere was getting close to breaking the lightspeed barrier. Whole reason I joined Exo proper was to get as close as I could once I finished my Extended Ed. Was even first officer on a couple of freighters before Edward's Spire. Figured there'd be conflict, even sabotage. I didn't expect things to escalate like they did."

"I don't think anyone did, sir. I've always wondered if what happened at Edward's Spire was supposed to be so catastrophic. Or even if it was Next Frontier that did it."

There was silence for a moment. Clayton knew the answer to that question, though he couldn't tell Castaño. Next Frontier had ordered the sabotage, though they tried to cover it up after the Spire collapsed, burying two hundred people. Enough of the data had been successfully scrubbed that it was difficult to glean the exact details, but he suspected that it had gone further than the executives had intended.

"You're probably right. I don't think anyone meant to plunge Zoar into war." Clayton paused, thinking. "I remember when I heard the news. We were on our way back down to Zoar from Selene. We'd brought up some fresh produce and a few other materials; Exosphere was still expanding its base there. We picked up a few workers to bring back for a couple months leave. I'd gone to high school with one of the guys. We were chatting in the chow hall when the captain came back and told us the news." Clayton shook his head, looking out absently at the steel beyond the transparent shell. "It was surreal. A couple minutes later we got footage of the Spire collapsing, straight down. Nobody could tear themselves away from it." He scoffed. "There was even a substantial deviation in our flight pattern that ended up costing the flight officer, captain and myself part of our checks." A moment passed in silence.

"I had just finished my flight tests," Castaño said, finally. "Went out to celebrate with some friends. We were having such a good time, we didn't see what was happening on the screen until we noticed that the whole bar had gone quiet. When I finally looked at it, it was all over. The tower was already a pile of rubble. Just dust and smoke."

"You lose anyone in the war?"

"No, not really. Most of my family lives further out. Not a lot of strategic sense in hitting a food source you share with the enemy."

"I suppose not." It was quiet and they both looked out at the grey interior of the bridge's shell.

"How about you, captain?" Castaño asked. "Did you lose anyone?"

"Yes." Clayton cleared his throat and looked left.

"I'm sorry. I didn't mean to pry."

"No, it's alright, lieutenant. I pried first. But we really don't know each other that well yet."

"Is it normal to know your subordinates well?" Castaño asked. "As captain of a ship, I mean. A few of my instructors at OTS taught that familiarity threatens discipline."

Clayton nodded. "To some extent. But there needs to be understanding. In the ancient days of Earth, the most powerful navies understood that a captain needed absolute authority if they were going to be out at sea for months or even years without easy access to their government for settling disputes. The captain needed to be just a step below God or the king. Things nowadays are ... surprisingly similar." Clayton chuckled. "I don't think we're ever going to be able to reinstitute lashings and the like, but the fact of the matter is ever since we broke the light barrier, communication is no longer faster than the ships themselves. This is more like Nelson's navy than anything that came after the telegraph or radio."

Clayton shook his head. "But that's a pretty long-winded answer. More simply put, lieutenant, I should be more like your father than your friend." He looked down at Castaño. "You weren't a rebellious child, were you?"

Castaño grinned. "I had my moments."

Clayton grinned back. "Well, I suggest you search the database for the cat o' nine tails before you talk back to me."

"That some kind of animal?"

Clayton chuckled. "Just look it up. And be glad you were born when and where you were."

The day after Mithril had their armor fitting, Goldman sidled up next to Kobayashi in the breakfast line "Something's up," he said.

"Is that so?"

They each finished filling their trays and turned to find a seat. "I don't trust Johansen." Goldman said, scanning the mess hall as they settled onto a bench.

"Just because she broke Allred's nose—"

"It's not that—she's up to something." Kobayashi raised an eyebrow and Goldman rolled his eyes and scooped a forkful of eggs onto his fork. "Okay, it's not like I've got hard evidence, but I'm telling you; no one that skilled and intelligent and, if her service record is anything to judge by, *driven* is going to be that disgruntled without trying to do something about it." Goldman's face was earnest. In place of his usual grin was a straight face, with penetrating blue eyes. Even when he stuffed the eggs in his mouth, it didn't lose the intensity.

"Like what?" Kobayashi asked.

"I don't know. But she's kept pretty specific company ever since she was assigned to the unit. I've talked with some Mithril, and they confirmed my own observations. She only seems to talk to Abramov and a few specific marines and navy personnel."

"So, she's reclusive."

Goldman shook his head. "I don't think that's it. I mean, look now, two tables behind me and to the left. Who's she sitting with?"

Kobayashi looked over Goldman's shoulder while he watched her face. "Abramov and two men from Alpha squad. Smith and Silver, I think. They're the only ones at that entire table." It was a long table and Kobayashi's platoon was not the only group of people in the mess hall. She met Goldman's eyes. He pointed his fork at her.

"Exactly. Major, if you don't believe me, watch them yourself."

"I've been watching." Goldman's eyebrows came together and he sat back. Kobayashi's lip twitched and she took a bite of gruel.

"So, you're not worried? Concerned at all?"

"I never said that."

Goldman exhaled. "Work with me here, major. I'm your XO; it'll help if we're on the same page."

Kobayashi straightened in her seat. "It's odd, sure. But I'm not going to jump to any conclusions. If I did, then I might suspect that you're up to something and just trying to throw me off the scent."

Goldman scoffed and crossed his arms, leaning back. "Oh, yeah? And what might I be up to?"

"Johansen's not the only one spending an inordinate amount of time with limited company."

"What do you mean? I make the rounds. Talk with all the marines."

"I've noticed you often arrive at PT coming from Navy NCO quarters, rather than your own." The color drained from his cheeks, and Kobayashi spooned some gruel into her mouth.

"I, uh..."

"What's her name, captain?"

"Do we really need to—"

"You said you wanted to be on the same page." Goldman swallowed and Kobayashi's lip twisted to the side. "There are no regulations against fraternization outside of the direct chain of command, captain. Not yet anyway." Kobayashi scraped her spoon against the bowl, gathering the last of the mealy cereal.

Goldman blushed but grinned. "I knew there was a sense of humor somewhere behind that stoic face." Kobayashi looked to the left.

"I watch everyone, captain," she said. "You keep your eye on Johansen. Let me know if you see something actionable."

"Yes, ma'am." He was still grinning as he shook his head. "Clearly, I could be more observant. I should have known I was going to get caught."

"Observant and discreet aren't the same."

Goldman scratched his head with one finger. "Understood, major."

"Do you really, or should I get you a dictionary?"

Goldman laughed. "I brought my own, actually. Not only does it put me to sleep at night, it's a better pillow than anything else on this state-of-the-art mausoleum." He made a show of looking around. "Seriously, what is with the Navy and all this white?"

Clayton's desk chirped and he set his tactile down. The black of the desk's projective surface was interrupted by a pulsing green circle. Clayton tapped it with a smile, and the green pulsed across the entire desk and as it dissipated, it was replaced with an ever so slightly out of focus projection of a chessboard. Across the desk, Amin materialized, smiling at Clayton.

"Good to see you again, captain."

Clayton returned the grin. "Likewise. Shall we?"

"Of course. My board, so you can pick."

"I'll take white."

Amin turned the board and Clayton looked at the pieces for a second, before tapping a pawn, then the space he wanted it to move to. He had never played a lot of chess and suspected that Amin had a great deal more experience. Given the set nature of the board and its variables, Clayton knew he was at a distinct disadvantage.

Amin responded with her own pawn. "So, how have you been settling into your new command?"

"Well enough. My senior staff seems perfectly competent, but there are always hiccups." Clayton made his move and Amin responded quickly. There was a short pause in conversation while they progressed further into the game.

"Any particular hiccups on your mind?"

Clayton grimaced, thinking of the report he'd received just that morning from Kobayashi through his first officer which detailed some concerns about Captain Johansen. And of course, his instinctive distrust of Spadt himself. Clayton moved a bishop out into the open.

"Only if you've got one of your own."

Amin smiled ruefully and took one of Clayton's pawns. "Well, it turns out we left dry dock with a shuttle already out of commission. The engine's shot to hell. No idea how it got past quality assurance."

Clayton chuckled and took one of Amin's pawns. "Sounds like somebody wasn't doing their job."

"What about you? What's your number one hitch so far?"

Clayton did not reply immediately. The board was starting to take shape. Amin's style was aggressive, just as her approach to conversation, it seemed. She'd already taken three of his pawns, driving hard into his front line. "Did Villeneuve brief you on my marine detachment?"

Amin nodded. "Major Kobayashi, right? Wasn't she the one who stopped the Presidents at Camp Coldwater?"

"That's the one. She's got concerns about her special ops commander, Captain Johansen." Clayton's bishop was in danger from one of Amin's knights. He slid it back.

"Oh? What happened?" Amin moved her knight deeper into Clayton's territory, providing him with an opportunity to take it. He didn't trust it.

"Johansen broke one of their pilots' noses during a sparring match. Which wouldn't be much of a concern except there have been a number of other, more minor incidents." Clayton gestured with an open hand and took Amin's knight with his own. Amin quickly took his knight with one of her rooks, giving it easy access to his queen.

"Is it across old corporate lines?" Amin asked.

Clayton looked at the board, shaking his head slightly. He should have seen that coming. "No. Allred, the pilot, didn't serve during the war. It's a discipline problem. The merger is still the best path forward." Taking her rook wouldn't remove his queen from danger; she had a pawn in position there, so Clayton moved a bishop in front of his queen.

"Something of an idealist, aren't you?"

"As naive as it sounds, I like to think of myself as a realist." Clayton saw an opportunity to take Amin's queen. It would take at least three turns to set up, depending on Amin's plans. He checked for any immediate blunders and moved a rook as the first phase of his trap.

"A realist whose reality certainly seems ideal."

"Zoar's had a single unified government ever since it was settled. One thousand years is a solid pattern; I'd like to see it continue." Clayton checked the board before moving his rook to the next position, threatening Amin's queen. He couldn't foresee any major developments that would upset his plan and so went forward with it.

"There were longer lasting empires brought to their knees back on Earth." Amin took the bait and captured his rook.

"Earth years were shorter than Zoar's." Clayton looked at the board longer than he needed too, before capturing a pawn with his bishop, threatening Amin's queen. "And besides, there was almost always an external aggressor as well as a failing government."

"Almost always." Amin took Clayton's bishop, and he immediately moved his knight to capture her queen.

"Almost. Sometimes it just took one or the other."

"An expensive victory, captain." Amin moved a pawn to capture his knight. Clayton didn't reply, instead taking a good hard look at the board. It was true. He still had one of each of his pieces, except his knights and about half of his pawns. Amin had still had both her rooks, her bishops and a knight, as well as most of her pawns, but as long as Clayton kept his wits about him, numbers alone wouldn't save Amin.

He pushed a pawn forward. "What would you say is the bigger problem for the Renovamen now? The government or the external threat?"

Amin looked up at Clayton, holding a knight. "Quite the question, captain."

"You had a point. There isn't a civilization in history that hasn't ended, and if the pattern holds, Zoar as we know it is on course for its end. So, are the aliens we're going to meet the Goths at the gate, or is the government rotting from the inside out?" Amin held Clayton's gaze for a moment before looking back at the board and completing her move.

"I think you can guess my position."

"Can I?" Clayton raised an eyebrow and smiled, moving his queen to take a pawn. "Check." Amin didn't reply, instead moving a bishop to defend her king, and Clayton took that as an invitation. "Maybe I will venture a guess." Clayton moved his queen out of danger. "Looking at the evidence so far, the aliens haven't been actively hostile. Given that the ship that took the Presidents was automated, we don't know that they intended to capture them. Beyond that, they were not in the Hathor system, but the Schweiz system, meaning that they likely have no idea where the Presidents originated. Two strikes against the Goths."

"And what about the rotting of our government?" Amin moved a rook into a position that compromised Clayton's queen and he was forced to move it to safety again.

"Well, we've just had the first major armed conflict in the history of the planet. Thaddeus Bear has installed himself as Director of the Fleet Integration program which echoes Caesar's rise to power, in my opinion. Rot takes a while, but I'd say the signs are there."

"I imagine there are other signs you see, captain." Amin moved a rook over a couple spaces.

Clayton nodded, looking at the board. He was missing something. What it was, he didn't know. "We discussed one yesterday using Admiral Villeneuve as a case study." He pushed his queen to threaten one of her knights.

"We did, didn't we? Maybe you are more of a realist than I gave you credit for. Regardless..." Amin grinned at him and moved the knight he had attacked with his queen. "Checkmate."

CHAPTER VIII

Shar'hre had been gone for hours. Fred had grown used to her regular and long absences and they made sense; his condition wasn't such that he needed constant attention, and it wasn't like he was going anywhere. Nevertheless, she normally returned by the time the sun began to set: twilight had already fallen. Fred limped restlessly back and forth in the dark hut. His leg had improved greatly, as had Shar'hre's patience with his frustration. He was grateful for her help, and he wished he could express it better. With a sigh, he sat down on his hammock and looked down at his bare feet on the dirt floor. Shar'hre had taken his shoes away after their first walk outside of the hut. Fred hadn't understood why, but he'd grown to like walking barefoot, not least because he'd had less difficulty walking since then. Not that correlation was causation. Fred looked up and saw some kind of glow coming through the yellow leaf wall of the hut. Shar'hre must be back.

He stood up and walked to the doorway. Stepping out, he looked down the road and was surprised to see that the glow was further away than he expected. It looked like a group of people carrying torches. He frowned but stayed where he was. He stood and watched them approach, arms crossed. As they grew closer, he saw that Shar'hre was leading the group. He relaxed, letting his arms drop to his sides. The group came within ten feet of Fred and stopped. Shar'hre continued towards him.

"What's going on?"

Shar'hre said something and pointed back the way they'd come. She turned to him and held out her arm. "Gumun." Uncertain, Fred stepped forward and wrapped his arm around her waist and she wrapped hers under his shoulders. They began to walk towards the group, which stood silently, parting to make way as Shar'hre and Fred came near. Fred was grateful for her support. He could walk on his own but any great distance. And (if he was being honest) the physical contact made things feel real. It made him feel real in a way he didn't surrounded by these strange people. They passed through the group and Fred noticed that most of them were as tall or taller than Shar'hre. Many carried spears and they all had axes strapped to their belts.

The group followed Shar'hre as she helped Fred down the dirt path. He felt as if all their eyes were on him. He couldn't help worrying about what was in store for him, and he tightened his arm around Shar'hre's waist. They walked in silence down the path. Eventually, Fred saw a pinprick of light up ahead. The road emerged abruptly from the forest and Fred found himself standing on the edge of what looked like a town or village, the road lined with torches.

The architecture here was highly reminiscent of Shar'hre's hut. While the buildings looked sturdier and most appeared to be significantly bigger, all were walled with the same yellow leaf weave as the hut, and few were taller. One notable exception rose twice as high. Standing across the road from a large clearing, it dominated the view. As they came further into the town, Fred felt the ground turn hard under his feet. Large stones of various shapes paved the road here, on the border of the clearing where Fred now saw a monument of some kind. It was ten or so feet tall, oblong, and nearly fifty feet long. Hefty, evenly-spaced fins protruded from it, giving the illusion of a square shape in the darkness. If not for that, Fred would've said it looked like an egg. It lay partially buried in the ground, nearly flat, but the smaller end was lifted about five feet up. Torches around the centerpiece reflected dully off it.

While Fred stared at the object, Shar'hre led him and their small procession around the monument. On the other side, the grassy area extended for another fifty feet. A crowd was gathered on the road beyond the grass. About ten feet out from the monument, two men and three women stood on a platform above the bonfire, facing the crowd. Two of the women were redheads, as were both of the men. The remaining woman had black hair and stood a pace behind them. Though all five were armed, Fred got the distinct impression that she was a guard of some kind.

Shar'hre led Fred towards the group by the bonfire. Most of the group that had followed them from the hut went off to join the crowd at the edge of the grass but two men continued with them. As they drew nearer, Fred began to distinguish the curly red hair and short beard of the taller of the two men; he was the one who had smeared that disgusting stuff all over Fred's face and spoken at Doctor Murdock's cremation. As they slowly climbed the wooden steps up the platform, however, Fred's eyes turned from him to the younger of the two redheaded women. She was the first person he'd seen who was shorter than him, although not by much.

And she was beautiful. A white circlet rested on her brow, a single red gem set into its center. Locks of dark red hair cascaded down her back, framing a freckled face. Her eyes looked brown but it was difficult to tell in the torchlight. Like the other redheads, the woman was dressed in beautiful blue and purple leaves, layered on top of each other in a way that made the colors shimmer in the torchlight. Unlike the tunics and skirts of leaves worn by the men and other women Fred had seen, this woman wore a full dress that reached almost to her ankles.

Fred looked up as Shar'hre came to a halt in front of the group. He glanced at the beautiful woman, only to find her looking at him. He was startled to see a magnificent amethyst in her eyes, rather than brown. A trick of the light? They were too vibrant and steady for that. The woman smiled at him and he realized she was younger than he had thought at first. He felt his cheeks grow warm and looked away.

Shar'hre let go of him unexpectedly and knelt in front of the group, bowing her head. Fred began to follow suit, awkwardly kicking his bad leg out behind him, but before he made it very far, he felt a hand on his shoulder. He looked back at the man who owned the hand. He shook his head, so Fred stopped and watched. The older man stepped forward. Now that he was closer, Fred could see faint wrinkles in the man's strong face and gray hairs in the red mane and beard. Like the shorter woman, he wore a circlet on his head, but unlike the younger woman's, his gleamed, reflecting the torchlight brightly enough that Fred couldn't tell what color it was, or if it was decorated with a stone like the woman's. He was close enough that Fred could see that his eyes were the same shade of purple as the woman's.

The man extended his left hand, palm down, speaking a few words. Shar'hre looked up and placed the back of her right hand in the man's palm. The man closed his fingers around her hand and lifted. Shar'hre stood slowly. Once she'd reached her full height, the man reached out with his right hand and cupped her cheek in his hand. Shar'hre spoke softly, dipping her head. The man nodded and stood back, smiling. It was fascinating. Fred was reminded of a scene he'd once seen from a play set on Earth. Ancient Europe, if he remembered correctly.

The taller, bearded man then stepped forward. A reverent look came over Shar'hre's face. She said something quietly. The man placed a hand on her shoulder and leaned forward, kissing her on the forehead. They exchanged a few words, glancing towards Fred. Fred fought the urge to shift onto his bad leg. What were they saying about him?

Then the man stepped past Shar'hre and approached Fred. Fred did his best not to shrink away from the man. He stood at least half a foot over Fred and was broad and muscled as well. Fred couldn't bring himself to meet the man's eyes, so he looked down.

The sword at the man's hip caught his eye, or rather, the pommel of the sword did.

A kite-shaped prism of translucent amethyst the size of a child's fist was set into the bottom of the hilt, held in place by four elegant gold spires that reached up the length of the rock at its edges. Two of the spires reached about half an inch past the jewel's end and curved to crescent moons, while the other spires stopped about a half an inch short. The spires' edges were curved and sharp. A deep red color swirled loosely through the stone, spreading apart like tendrils of blood in water away from the hilt of the sword. A faint blue ribbon danced around the red. The swirls faded into the amethyst as they spread towards the point framed by the golden spires. While the edges of the stone were set into the gold spires and appeared rounded, the point in the center looked vicious. The stone was both violence and elegance, fire and water. If it were natural, it was unlike any precious stone Fred had seen.

The man began to speak and Fred was jolted out of his reverie. He looked up at the man who was pointing a single finger at Fred's chest, saying Fred's name. Then he placed his finger on his own chest, speaking slowly and enunciating carefully.

"Hrin-tar Ty-green." He paused, looking at Fred expectantly.

Fred pointed at himself. "I'm Fred," he said. He pointed at the man. "And you're Hrintar?" Hrintar nodded and drew his sword. It rasped as it scraped against the scabbard. Fred involuntarily stepped back, but found the space already occupied by the man who had stopped him from bowing earlier. Hrintar took another step towards Fred, who swallowed and managed to look past the sword at Shar'hre who was still watching Hrintar with that same reverent look. Then Hrintar knelt and bowed his head, spinning the sword in the same motion so he held the blade in both hands, the handle pointing up towards Fred. Fred stood for a moment, trying to understand what was happening.

Then he grasped the worn hilt, lifting the heavy sword out of Hrintar's hands. Despite its weight, it felt good in Fred's hand. Balanced. He held it in front of his face. The steel (or that's what he assumed it was) was bright and untarnished. It looked wicked sharp on both edges. While the blade tapered from the handle, the tip bulged out subtly before coming to a point. There were a few notches in the blade's edges and innumerable scratches on both flat sides. It had been used. Extensively. The cross guard was simple: a black metal formed a "T" with sharp edges on small, upward spikes where both guards came to their ends.

Fred realized that Hrintar was still kneeling in front of him, head bowed. Feeling a little foolish and like he must be in some kind of dream, Fred lowered the flat of the blade, tapping Hrintar on one shoulder, then the other, before holding the sword up again. Hrintar stood from his kneeling position. Unsure of what to do next, Fred paused for a moment before turning the sword sideways, resting the blade in both hands, offering it back to Hrintar. He took it and turned to face the expectant crowd. Heat rushed through Fred, and he started to itch. He'd probably messed that up. What was he thinking? Knighting someone? Some relief came when Hrintar raised the sword into the air with one hand and addressed the crowd.

He was forceful and charismatic. Fred couldn't follow the speech, though he was able to pick out a few words. Trying to follow it made him sleepy, like his early days of Spanish immersion, just before comprehension had really started to come to him. Hrintar was still speaking when Shar'hre came to Fred's side and wrapped an arm around him, nodding to the stairs off the stage. Fred nodded and put his arm around her waist, and they slipped away.

No one followed as they left the town, headed back the way they'd come. Fred didn't realized how exhausted he was until they were well into the forest and it dropped on him like a sack of potatoes. He leaned even more heavily on Shar'hre but did his best to hold himself up. Each step seemed like two and Fred began to think he would fall asleep while he walked.

When they finally reached the hut, Fred collapsed in his hammock, only vaguely aware of Shar'hre climbing into her own as he fell first into a deep lull, then a full sleep.

Shar'hre lay in her hammock, looking up at the ceiling as she processed the ceremony. Hred had truly honored the Tuluchur. And yet... Shar'hre looked at Hred. He was already asleep. He seemed so small and vulnerable. She could not shake that from her mind, nor his hesitation before initiating the *golhum*. And it was a *golhum* unlike any other she had seen. When one offered a blade to another it was expected to be accepted. To deny by dropping or throwing the weapon away was the greatest mark of disrespect. But to accept and return the blade, the blade the held *Narssarn*, no less: what did that mean?

Shar'hre studied Hred's face. He was deep in the peace of sleep, and it dawned on her; the Telahren did not need a weapon. A messenger such as he did not need to be a warrior in the manner of the Meltesh. If war came, he would have at his disposal something more powerful than a sword. The stories of the Jeli'ahsh told of incredible tools and of weapons that could kill or stop a foe in their tracks in the blink of an eye. Hred had accepted Hrintar's oath but did not need the weapon. It also meant that though Hred was Telahren, Hrintar remained Tuluchur; he was still needed to lead the Meltesh through the *Hroonun*.

The Hroonun. She did not understand her place in it. Why had Hrintar chosen her to be his lee'inkah? She was a simple healer. He would have done well to choose *Shashay* Farloa. She held the stature to be the *fiyal* of a Tuluchur. Stranger still was the length of their engagement. Perhaps Hrintar desired to braid his hair before they Joined, but the fact remained that he offered little more warmth to her than to any of his followers.

Shar'hre turned in her hammock, setting it to swing. Despite her active thoughts, her eyelids grew heavy. Whatever her or Hred's place in the Hroonun, she trusted the Tuluchur to bring them through it. She glanced over at Hred one last time. Satisfied that he still slept soundly, she laid back and closed her eyes. All would be well.

Fred woke up as he fell out of the hammock, opening his eyes just in time to see the dirt floor rushing up to meet him. He thumped into the ground and the panic subsided as he realized he was awake. Aching, he tried to push himself up, but the ground refused to cooperate. At first he thought he must have smacked his head and got a concussion, but after a moment he realized that the ground was really and truly shaking. Hard. It was the third such quake since he had met Hrintar. With the frequency, Fred was beginning to understand why these people preferred short, easily raised buildings to more permanent structures. Feeling a bit sick, Fred decided to stay put until the world returned to normal. It was unlikely that anything heavy would fall on him.

When the ground finally stopped shaking, Fred pushed himself up to stand. Looking around, he saw that nothing was out of place and Shar'hre wasn't in the hut. He stepped through the leaf curtain that led outside. The sun peeked just over the trees to his right and twilight was descending. Looking east, Fred saw a figure coming toward him—probably Shar'hre. She normally returned well before dark, but he imagined the quake had slowed her down. He started towards her. It wasn't far, though his leg still had some mending to do. Despite the gathering darkness, he was able to confirm that it was indeed Shar'hre as he drew near.

He raised his hand in greeting. "Hiyah."

Shar'hre waved back. "Hiyah, Hred. A'u chu?"

"Aym goot." As he'd pieced more and more of the language together, Fred had been relieved to find that the language was similar to English. It made lapsing into his native tongue more common than he had when he was studying Spanish, but it was a small price to pay for easier comprehension. He'd made good progress in the past week or so. He missed having grammatical reference on hand, but his immersion was so complete here that it more than made up for it. Additionally, he'd put a great deal more effort in after the strange ceremony with Hrintar and Shar'hre seemed eager to teach him.

"Tish laed. Wusho ath."

"Yeah, wush." Together they turned and made their way back to the hut. Ahead of them, the last blue of twilight was deepening to black over the tree line. It was a quiet sight and it seemed as if the quake had never occurred. They walked in silence and Fred wondered what Shar'hre was thinking. Was she as moved to stillness by the vista as he was?

It was fully dark when they reached the hut. As they turned to go inside, Fred heard a rustle in the trees behind them. He turned to look but felt strong hands pushing him away, into the hut. Caught off balance, he tumbled to the ground inside the door. He scrambled to his feet, heard Shar'hre shout outside. He rushed back out. He couldn't make out anything but thought he saw a flicker of movement to his right. He turned towards it, just as something jammed into his gut.

Fred doubled over, gasping for breath, and felt rough hands yank his arms back and tie them behind his back. Then, someone was jabbing him in the back with something hard. He started walking forward and the prodding lessened. He continued walking, straining to make out the aggressors but couldn't see more than the suggestion of movement. His mind raced. Who were these people? Where was Shar'hre? Where were they taking him and why? No answers were forthcoming, and Fred felt it better not to ask. He wouldn't be understood, even if they seemed like they might answer his questions.

Fred's leg grew sore, but they marched on, seemingly forever. As they walked, Fred became more and more aware of the sounds around him. Most prominent were the constant snapping of twigs and brushing of branches on the party, but Fred could make out breathing as well. There had to be at least four or five, but Fred figured there could be more. Occasionally one of Fred's captors would grunt a brief question or direction and be answered in kind. The thought of making a break for it crossed his mind, but it was pure fantasy. Even with a good leg, he doubted he could outrun any of these people.

Finally, after what Fred guessed was at least two hours of constant walking, he could make out firelight ahead. His leg burned, but he did his best not to stumble or drag it. As they got closer to the fire, he was able to make out the people around him. He counted seven, not including the one prodding him along from behind. In front of him, two men held Shar'hre by the arms, despite her hands being tied like his own. The rest of their escort was spread along the path around them, each carrying spears and wearing axes on their belts.

Ahead, the source of the firelight came into view. The fire illuminated a small clearing. Beds of wide, frond-like leaves were scattered around it. A small canopy of leaves hung between a few trees to the left of the fire. As they approached the fire, two people emerged from beneath the canopy. They (like everyone on the planet) were tall and fierce looking. A dark-haired man stood in front of a blonde woman. Unlike the men around him, he had a sword, though it was nowhere near as ornate as the one Hrintar carried. His massive arms were crossed, and he looked at the approaching group with a hard face. The woman wore a similar expression. Both were taller than even the average person among these giants.

The group approached the pair and pushed Fred and Shar'her to their knees. Fred looked at Shar'hre. She looked alright, though he thought he could see the beginning of a bruise on her cheek and her usually impeccable braid was coming out. She stared up at the two who stood above them, then spoke.

"Kahsh!" She bent forward and spit on the man's sandaled feet. The man stared at Shar'hre for a second, then pulled back an open hand, clearly to hit Shar'hre. Fred sat up, off his haunches and the man looked at him, hand still raised. Fred met his gaze, but after a moment sank back onto his heels. Suddenly aware of his heart pounding, Fred focused on his breathing. It wouldn't do to provoke these people. He looked at Shar'hre who had yet to look away from the man.

Out of the corner of his eye, Fred saw the giant woman put a hand on the man's shoulder. He lowered his hand and both of them stared at Fred. The man spoke, but it was too fast for Fred to pick anything out. The man continued to look at Fred for a moment before he barked in laughter and gestured to Fred, saying something else, after which all of the kidnappers laughed. The woman moved past the man and approached Fred. Now that she was in full view, Fred saw the unmistakable belly of a late-term pregnancy. She reached Fred and crouched down, grabbing him by the chin. He pulled away, but her grip was strong and she held his face in front of her, looking at Shar'her as she spoke.

"Kah?" This Fred understood. Judging by its use, he figured it must be a pretty strong insult. "Genit Tygreen ishent kah. Ish kah. Telahren?" With a scoff, the woman gave Fred's chin a wag and stood. She continued speaking, looking out at the crowd. Fred did his best to glean some meaning from the short speech but couldn't decipher any more than the occasional word. Tygreen was repeated several times, sometimes attached to Genit. Fred remembered that Hrintar had used Tygreen as part of his name. Was Genit a person then? A relative of Hrintar's? Fred glanced between the man and the woman standing above him, then at Shar'hre who glared at them. Was one of them Genit? Hrintar had seemed to honor Fred. If they were related, why would they kidnap him and why would Shar'hre despise them?

The woman stopped speaking and the man nodded to the people behind Shar'hre and Fred. Someone grabbed him by the shoulders and dragged him to his feet. Others surged around them and began to tear down the camp. Fred shook out his weak leg. It looked like they would be walking through the night.

Shar'hre strained against her bindings. It was a fruitless endeavor. Even were she able to free her hands, she could not escape her captors and she certainly could not defeat them. If she was alone she would try to escape, but she could not leave Hred. He was her charge. He was Telahren. Perhaps even her friend, despite the few words they shared. She looked over her shoulder at him. Even under the cover of the forest she was able to pick out the outline of his face and the form of his gait, both of which seemed normal. At least his leg was not slowing him so much that Genit's men harassed him.

Shar'hre felt a rough hand on her shoulder and heard a gruff voice. "Turn around. Stop looking at the *ayahreh*." Sha'hre bristled.

She straightened and forced eye contact with the man. "He is Telahren. He is not a fraud."

The man laughed. "I have never met a stupid no'ihrah. Your Tuluchur must swing your hammock like ocean waves."

Shar'hre flushed but before she could reply, she heard another voice over her shoulder. "Quiet, Hathrum. Many follow Hrintar; despite his transgressions, he is wise." Shar'hre looked at the speaker. To her surprise, it was the same woman who had given that speech before they had been marched along. She had never met her before but from what little Hrintar had told her about Genit, she guessed this was his wife, Gal'Leah.

Hathrum bowed his head. "Yes. Of course, *Wolbaun*."

"There may be merit in some of his teachings." Gal'Leah stepped up alongside Shar'hre and her guards. She had one hand on her swollen belly. Shame flooded Shar'hre's gut and she hunched, grimacing. Why? She had no reason to be ashamed of what she thought of these heretics. They had kidnapped her and the Telahren! They had no honor. She swallowed and straightened up. She did not look at Gal'Leah, but she couldn't stop her thoughts from returning to the woman and the life growing in her.

Why had she joined her husband on this venture so late in her term? Shar'hre had always supported the practice of easing the woman's burden as pregnancy advanced, though a few women she had tended had insisted on working as hard as ever. It was something she respected, though she considered it foolhardy. She glanced at Gal'Leah and guilt burned anew in her stomach. She gave her head a small shake. She could not afford to sympathize with these people.

Dawn was coming by the time they cleared the forest and found themselves on the outskirts of a village. Fred's head was clouded and his leg was completely numb. They had only stopped a couple times during their march, leading Fred to suspect that they expected to be followed by Hrintar and forces loyal to him. But why? Why were Hrintar and Genit so invested in Fred? He was nothing special. He was a shrimp compared to all these people, he didn't speak the language, and knew nothing about the world he was on, let alone the people native to it. The only notable thing about him was his arrival on the planet. Did they think he had advanced technology they could use? They would be sorely disappointed if that were the case. He was no scientist or engineer.

As they marched further into the village, Fred found himself dully surprised to hear children's voices. Looking beyond the guard in front of him, he saw two little girls chasing each other in the road. Apparently, village life started early. Looking around, Fred saw adults emerging from their broad-leaf huts, watching the procession with crossed arms. A man hurried out into the road, speaking with a scolding voice as he picked up one of the girls and took the other by the hand.

The group moved past where the man stood with the girls and Fred looked at the one that sat in the crook of the man's arm, sucking her thumb. Her eyes were green with the characteristic slitted pupils of these people. Her hair was blonde, and her skin's changing tones lay on each other like layered brushstrokes. She pulled her thumb out of her mouth and waved at Fred, who could only smile wearily and raise his elbow, his wrists chafing against the bindings. The guard behind Fred gave him a jab in the back with the butt of his spear and the man holding the girl pulled her hand down, scolding her again.

The group continued a little further before turning down a side path toward a large hut. It looked sturdier than most of the others, with corners of large, living trees that were surprisingly straight, considering all the trees Fred had seen. They slowed down suddenly. Looking forward, he watched as the front of the group parted, taking up positions along the side of the hut. Ahead of him, the man and woman who seemed to be in charge continued on, through the leaf flaps into the hut. Fred's guard steered him into the hut behind them.

Fred entered dumbly. His eyelids were growing heavy, and it was all he could do to keep his head up. He was only vaguely aware of the cord around his wrists being untied. Someone wrapped their arm under his shoulders, supporting and Fred's arm automatically found it's way around her waist and he and rolled to lean heavily on her. His head lolled and he snapped his eyes open. In front of him was a hammock and Shar'hre lowered him into it. He was asleep before he could lift his legs in after him.

Shar'hre woke up to someone shaking her arm. She opened her eyes to see Gal'Leah standing over her. She blinked groggily, forcing herself to put together the pieces of what had happened before she fell asleep.

Gal'Leah gave her little time. "Come, No'ihrah."

Shar'hre looked across the room at Fred, who was still sleeping. "I will not leave the Telahren."

Gal'Leah closed a hand around Shar'hre's arm. "It is not a request." Shar'hre tried to pull away, but Gal'Leah pulled up hard, dragging Shar'hre out of bed. Shar'hre was barely able to swing her knees out so she did not slam into ground on her side. "You have my word that he will not be harmed." Shar'hre stumbled to her feet, and Gal'Leah gave her no opportunity to gain her footing before pulling her out the door. One of her cronies grabbed Shar'hre's other arm. Together they steered her down the road through town and into another mah.

Inside the mah was an old woman, someone Shar'hre recognized from somewhere. Wavy, silver hair fell unbraided around her shoulders, and she stood tall, holding herself with a strength that denied her wrinkled and leathery skin. Her hredahsh was unusual, consisting of hundreds, perhaps thousands of round, dark marks. The old woman gestured to Shar'hre, looking past her. Gal'Leah stepped in front of Shar'hre and undid her bindings. It was then that Shar'hre recalled the old woman. She almost could not believe it. She looked at Gal'Leah, who smirked and pushed her forward. Shar'hre stepped forward.

The old woman met Shar'hre's gaze and nodded. "Welcome, No'ihrah. I am sorry you were brought here in this manner. I would have preferred a different approach. My nephew, however, has always tended toward brutish behavior."

"*Shahsh* Ema'eln. What is happening? Why are you here, with these..." Shar'hre trailed off. She did not want to suggest that a woman of Ema'eln's stature would throw in with kidnappers and warmongers.

"*Dahdlah*," Ema'eln said, her voice soft, "you do not know the whole story. Hrintar has wronged Genit as much Genit or myself have wronged him." Shar'hre stiffened but Ema'eln continued before she could speak. "Believe his teachings if you will, but my grandson has long resented me. I did not give him the Sword of Garither. He took it while I slept, later claiming a blessing from the Jeli'ahsh. That is not the way of the blade."

Shar'hre shook her head. "If it was the will of the Jeli'ahsh—"

"Do not preach to me!" Ema'eln's voice was quiet but carried enough anger that Shar'hre stepped back involuntarily. "Neither the Meltesh nor their deities have any right to dictate the course of that sword; it was handed down from *Ay Caitan* to *Ay Caitan* of Garither from the founding of the country forward. As the last *Ay Caitan* of Garither, it is my brother's descendants who hold first right to the sword." Ema'eln sighed and her eyes drifted from Shar'hre. "Be it an honor or a burden." She refocused on Shar'hre. "Hrintar has always coveted it. More so when Valatiy refused it." Shar'hre swallowed, her mind racing. Could that be true? How could Ema'eln, the hero who turned back the Hrar'ihcohrean invasion, contradict the teachings of the Tuluchur? Her own grandson? Did she not believe in the Jeli'ahsh at all?

"But what of the Telahren?" She asked. "He accepted Hrintar's *golhum* and gave the sword back. Does that mean nothing?"

Ema'eln shook her head. "Your Telahren does not even speak our tongue. What can a dumb messenger accomplish? He cannot know what his actions mean, even if his presence heralds the Meltesh *Hroonun*."

Shar'hre swallowed and looked away. She had asked herself that question before and she still had no answer. She shifted her weight from one leg to the other. Hrintar could not be lying. If he were a false prophet, what did that mean about all the beliefs Shar'hre held? She could not extricate them from Hrintar's teachings without leaving a great hole. His were the only teachings that explained death and life, that addressed what Shar'hre saw in dying and newborn eyes.

Ema'eln interrupted Shar'hre's thoughts, putting a hand on her shoulder. "I believe my grandson to be a good man, *dahdlah*. He may even be the prophet you and others believe him to be. Were it not for his ambition, we would have no quarrel. All Genit and I want is to restore the Narssarn to its rightful owner. You and this Telahren are not prisoners here. Bringing you here ensures that both sides of the story are heard. You are free to return to Gid'Del, but I would be pleased if you stayed and gave me the opportunity to get to know my future granddaughter." Shar'hre looked up at Ema'eln, her heart palpitating. Ema'eln smiled. "News of the

Tuluchur spreads quickly. Every soul in Meen knows that he has taken a young no'ihrah as his lee'inkah. Who else would he trust to care for his messenger?"

Shar'hre looked down then and a thought occurred to her. "If you wanted to tell your side of the story, why kidnap us?"

Ema'eln looked down at her hands. "That was not my choice. Hrintar does not trust me. After his mother died, I raised him. Our relationship has always been strained. When I expressed a desire to meet this Telahren, he turned me away and Keem Uahrey judged that I should not interfere. Genit grew impatient and took matters into his own hands."

Shar'hre looked at Ema'eln, her mind racing. Hrintar had told her very little about himself. She recalled in one of his sermons he spoke of his mother's death, during the Invasion. She had not realized his father had also died. She did not know her lee'inkah at all. "We will stay for a time." She looked back at Ema'eln. "But I have your word? We can leave whenever we want?"

"Yes. I only ask that when you leave, you tell Keem Uahrey that we want an audience with him. Though Hrintar has the King's ear, I believe you presenting our request will give him cause to consider our case."

Shar'hre nodded. "As you wish."

Ema'eln smiled. "Good. Now, you must be hungry. We will prepare a meal and wake your *dehihrah* when it is ready."

Fred woke, feeling different but not much less tired. It was as if the suffocating fog that had permeated his mind had ebbed to the back of his head; it lingered but didn't dominate his mind. After a moment, he noticed that his legs were fully in the hammock. Shar'hre must've put them in after he passed out. Fred realized that it was lighter in the hut than it had been when he fell asleep. He must have slept through most of the morning. His stomach growled and his hunger caught his attention.

Yawning, he sat up and looked around the hut. The other hammock was empty and Shar'hre was nowhere to be seen. Fred tensed at the realization that he was in enemy territory, alone. He found himself gripping the edge of the hammock and forced a deep breath. She probably wasn't far. Their captors had not mistreated them so far, beyond kidnapping them and marching them through the night, anyway. And they had removed their restraints; there was no reason to suspect that anything had happened to her. Or that anything was going to happen to him, for that matter.

Fred stood and took a step toward the door. His leg burned in protest, but Fred pushed on, ignoring it. It was just sore. His whole body was, really, which put things in perspective. He lifted the flap and stepped outside, anticipation rising in his chest, though he told himself there was no reason to worry. Outside, a couple of men spoke near an open area where a group of children ran in a mass. Looking closer, Fred realized they were kicking something around. A ball?

He stepped out further. One of the men glanced at him but returned to his conversation immediately. No one seemed concerned by his presence now. Looking around, Fred saw no sign of Shar'hre or any of the people who had captured him. It occurred to him that even in his state, they should have posted a guard. Another wave of anxiety washed through him. What was going on? He looked around again and, still seeing no one else, he limped over to the two men. They looked at him as he approached. One addressed him, but Fred only caught a couple words, meaningless without context. He took a deep breath and assembled the best sentence he could.

"Haer hisht Shar'hre?" One of the men sniggered and the other grinned. Fred flushed. He knew he was a long way from fluent, but that didn't take the sting out of his ignorance. Shar'hre was the only person he'd ever spoken with. One of the men took pity on him and pointed down the road. Fred paused and followed his finger. Which hut specifically? Or was it out of town, in the forest?

He looked back at the man and nodded hesitantly. "Thanks." The man returned the nod and Fred started down the road slowly, searching for some sign of Shar'hre, or even Genit or the pregnant woman from the night before. He reached the first hut and paused outside of it. What if Shar'hre wasn't inside? How would the people inside react? He looked back at the men, who had returned to their conversation.

Fred pushed the leaf door aside and peered in. Two women stood with their backs to him, working at a table against the far side of the hut. One's hair was silver and unbraided, the other dark and thickly braided. Fred stepped inside gingerly.

"Shar'hre?"

The women both turned and Fred was relieved to see that the dark-haired woman was Shar'hre. The smile on her face surprised and relieved him. She crossed the hut towards him, sidestepped a low table, and hugged him. Fred welcomed the embrace, confused though he was.

Shar'hre let him go. "Tish ay, Hred." She gestured to the older woman who had stepped away from the table. "h'Shish Ema'eln Tygreen." The woman kicked her chin up at Fred. He dropped his own briefly in a greeting. Her blue eyes skipped over him and Fred almost shivered. Something about that look told him that she had evaluated him and found him wanting. In what specifically, he didn't know, but the vigor she radiated just standing made him feel inadequate. He straightened his shoulders.

"Shish eahro, woom uf graed hrespah." Shar'hre said slowly. Although Fred didn't recognize every word, he was able to decipher most of the meaning. As if it wasn't obvious from the way she carried herself, this Ema'eln was clearly a person of importance and standing among these people. Though she wore none of the purple colors of Uahrey's entourage and their meeting lacked the circumstance of his meeting with the Keem, she seemed every bit as royal.

"Shish doo Hrintarsha gramma," Shar'hre continued, her voice quiet, almost hushed. Conflicted, Fred thought. As he sorted through the sentence, he cocked an eyebrow. If this was Hrintar's grandma, why had they been grabbed in the middle of the night? Had he been caught up in some kind of family drama? If so, what was Genit's role? Fred looked from Shar'hre to Ema'eln. Maybe "gramma" was a false cognate.

Fred bowed his head again as Ema'eln came near. "Aym Fred Cooper," he said.

"Aynoh." Ema'eln extended her hand and grasped Fred by his forearm. A handshake of sorts, which surprised Fred; no one else had engaged him in a physical greeting like this. "Chewar Telahren, aymalld."

Fred tilted his head to the side, biting the inside of his lip. He still didn't know exactly what "Telahren" meant. But the word always accompanied his name, and he guessed there must be some significance to it beyond simply "stranger," given how he'd been treated. It was almost ... reverent. He didn't like it. Whatever status these people had elevated him to, it was one he was unprepared for and unworthy of.

"Aymchalld Telahren, bud..." Fred's eyes flicked around the room as he searched for the words. Unable to find them, he gestured aimlessly. Ema'eln's lips pulled up slightly at the corners and she addressed Shar'hre, too quickly for Fred to pick out much. Shar'hre responded in kind and although Fred did his best to pick it apart, he was unable to keep up with the speed, even if he had the vocabulary necessary to follow it. After some more back and forth (from which Fred was able to discern that things were agreeable, if not fully settled) Ema'eln addressed him again.

"Chewar gudihush." She gestured toward the low table. "Cheweed thuh mee." Fred glanced at Shar'hre who nodded and moved past him to rejoin Ema'eln at the table at the back of the hut. Fred settled into a cross legged position at the low table.

"His Meltish is better than I was led to believe." Ema'eln opened a jar of *huyshra* and took a pinch out, adding it to the large bowl of groop that Shar'hre was stirring. Hred sat behind them at the table.

"I think it is better than he realizes."

"With some work, he will control it in short order."

"Did it take you long?"

"Yes. It was many changes of the moons before I did not fumble with your language. It is a softer tongue than Raricorean and it took me time to get used to it."

"Would you help me teach him?"

There was a short pause before Ema'eln nodded. "I will. For as long as you stay with us." She looked down into the groop. "I think it is ready."

Shar'hre nodded. The groop had thickened sufficiently. Much more and it would be too viscous to take through a straw. She set the spoon aside and picked up the bowl. She and Ema'eln joined Hred at the table.

As Ema'eln passed wooden straws around the table, Fred looked into the bowl. "This … is groop? Like Shar'hre…" He trailed off, rolling his wrists with open hands, searching for a word.

"Like I make?" Shar'hre asked. "Like Shar'hre makes?"

Hred nodded. "Like Shar'hre makes. Like you … make." He put his straw into the bowl, but before he could put his lips around it, Ema'eln pulled it away from him. Hred looked up at Ema'eln with a furrowed brow. She took his hand and Shar'hre's and leaned forward, head bowed.

"From land to land, on one side of the River and the other, might we ever be sustained. In the mortal world and beyond, may family and friends sit and break bread with us." She looked up and saw Shar'hre's surprised face.

"What was that?"

"A prayer, dahdlah, from my own land. I may be long gone from it, but it will never be fully gone from me." Her mouth turned up at the corners, but there was a sadness in her voice and eyes for a brief moment. Then Ema'eln looked from Shar'hre to Hred and back, smiling more fully. "Now, eat. Eat!"

When the groop hit Shar'hre's tongue she closed her eyes and sighed. She had noticed differences in Ema'eln's recipe while they prepared it, but she had not expected it to be so good. It did not have quite the same bite but was slightly more bitter.

She swallowed and looked across the table at Hred, pleased to see that his reaction was similar to her own. He released his lips from the straw and swallowed, his face relaxed in a slight smile of satisfaction.

"Do you like it?" Ema'eln asked. Hred looked at her for a second before nodding.

"It is good," he said. His mouth remained open for a moment and his eyes shifted to a point behind her. Then he sighed and shrugged.

"Delicious? Tasty?" Ema'eln asked, rubbing her stomach with one hand.

Hred smiled. "Delicious," he said, patting his own stomach. "Delicious."

CHAPTER IX

It is also worth pointing out just how fractious the people of Earth were prior to its destruction. Politically, spiritually, culturally. A plethora of nations and subcultures, such that within a given nation (particularly prosperous ones) there was little agreement of what was important. Some said this religion, others said that religion. Others said this kind of music and still others said this or that sport, or leader, or political ideology. There was a rise in what might be called cult worship that eroded and denied camaraderie in favor of shared opinion and experience.

—From "Why Now?" by Tobin Gorokhov

"Coming out of the corridor in ten, sir."

"Very well." Clayton nodded, hands clasped behind his back as he surveyed the bridge. It bustled with activity. Astrogators and other specialists moved around the mission pods behind Clayton, checking figures and readings, while below him, Castaño and the other station heads prepared to exit the corridor. Spadt sat stiffly in his chair below and left of Clayton, monitoring the bridge just as Clayton did. The cameras on the shell had been activated and swirling violet and white light illuminated the bridge.

Once they picked up the Presidents, it would be a few more days in the corridor before they arrived in the Schweiz System but this rendezvous would give the crew a break from the monotony of FTL travel. All of them had assignments that kept them busy, but a breath of fresh air was always nice. Clayton himself was glad for a change of pace. Aside from a game of chess every so often with Captain Amin, there was little to break up his day-to-day routine.

"Five minutes to corridor exit, captain."

"Understood." Clayton settled into his seat. "Commander Spadt, sound general alert: prepare for FTL corridor departure."

"Aye, sir." Spadt did not look at Clayton, instead opening a channel to the entire ship. "All hands, prepare for FTL transition. Departments, run checklists." He closed the channel.

"Lieutenant Jones, sitrep on our tactical systems."

"All green, commander."

"Commander Dixon?" Here he looked down to the woman sitting beside Castaño in the belly of the bridge.

"All departments and off-duty personnel report readiness, commander."

Spadt turned to Clayton. "All hands prepared, captain."

"Thank you, commander. Lieutenant Castaño, you have full control."

"Aye, sir: full control. Dropping out in three minutes. Better buckle up."

Clayton grinned. The jolt of dropping out of the corridor wasn't enough to throw someone from their seat. It wasn't even as bad as landing a shuttle, but it still unsettled Clayton's stomach. As he waited for the drop, he wondered what he was going to have on his hands when they picked up the Presidents. The three of them had been alone together for a month, and that was following the abduction of the rest of their team. That was enough to mess with anyone's psyche.

"Entry into normal space in ten, nine..." Castaño began the count and Clayton shifted in his seat, holding the armrests. "Three, two, one, mark!" The ship's engines whined and the white outside the cockpit changed suddenly to black. The ship shuddered once, Clayton's stomach dropped, and it was over. Outside, a swath of the galaxy was exposed to Clayton and his crew. Without the interference of any nearby stellar bodies the empty blackness was marked with a myriad of bright stars.

"Report, lieutenant."

Clayton could see Castaño smiling in satisfaction below him. "I'm picking up the signal buoy, right where it should be, ten kilometers ahead. The President's ship's FID tag is hovering there too."

"Set an intercept course. Commander Dixon, send a greeting and request a sitrep from them."

"Aye, sir."

"Lieutenant Jones, tactical report."

"Everything's quiet out there, sir. All systems..." he paused. Clayton looked at his tactical officer's back, but Spadt beat him to the question.

"Something wrong, lieutenant?"

"No, sir. There was a brief interruption in security protocols on C deck, but it's settled now. Probably a hiccup in protocol transition between FTL and normal space."

"Run thorough diagnostics, lieutenant. Get it fixed," Spadt said. Clayton caught Spadt's eye and nodded in approval. He needed to mend their relationship; Spadt was too good of an officer for Clayton to continue letting his natural distrust get the better of him.

"Aye, sir," Jones said.

"Captain, we are receiving a message from the Presidents," Dixon said.

"Go ahead, commander."

"They are reporting green and requesting to meet with you upon their arrival."

"Acknowledged. Instruct them to land in Hangar A; I'll meet them there." Clayton stood and looked at Spadt. "You have the bridge, commander. Once the Presidents are docked, begin preparations for FTL."

"Aye, sir. I have the bridge." As Clayton made for the door, Spadt stood and moved to take his seat. Clayton almost turned around. He stopped himself just short. He needed to trust his first officer.

The shuttle *Momma Bear* came through the airlock above Clayton, descending to eye level and then below the catwalk. It was massive for a shuttle; it had to be, in order to house twenty people for six months. Before leaving Zoar, Clayton had transferred four of his issued short-range shuttles before they left Gibraltar Station to accommodate it. In many ways, the bulky *Grizzly* class ship was every bit as impressive as *Trafalgar* and the other Nelson-classes. The shuttle's FTL engine was the smallest ever designed, compressed into a cubic space that rested on top of the ship, between its cockpit and "shoulders." As it came to rest on the floor of the hangar, Clayton saw the mild resemblance to the ship's ancient, Earth bear namesake.

He heard a loud puff of air as he started down the stairs; the ship depressurizing itself. Clayton reached the hangar floor and the ship's ramp descended. Before it had touched down, two figures started down it. The one in gold armor stood taller than the one in blue, but it was the one in blue who grabbed Clayton's attention. Her face was pinched together, her whole body pulled tight to itself as she strode down the ramp. Clayton couldn't tell if it was anger or determination that constricted her and drove her forward. Either would make sense. The man's expression was neutral and his gait calm, but Clayton suspected it was a facade. They made a beeline for Clayton.

The man in gold extended his hand and Clayton shook it. "Captain Clayton, C-Wo Larson." Larson gestured to Hale. "This is Mac-Wo Hale."

"Have the doys figured anything out from our report?" Hale asked. Straight to the point: not surprising, even without reading her dossier. If Clayton had been stuck four weeks without knowing what had happened to his squad mates and unable to do anything about it, he would want answers too.

"Nothing actionable, but we're working on it. If we can get the data you weren't able to transmit through the relays, that would help."

"Lead the way, sir."

"Of course." Clayton nodded and turned to the lead the way out of the hangar.

When the ship dropped out of the corridor, Kobayashi was in her quarters, sitting straight up on the edge of her bunk. The rendezvous with the Presidents was happening during personal hours for the marines. Kobayashi stood and walked the short length of the room, up next to the door where the small table and two chairs stood and back to the head of her bunk. She had enough room to engage in a variety of body weight training between her desk and bed. A personal lavatory was attached to the room as well. A small space, but one that fulfilled all Kobyashi's necessities.

She walked the length of the room again, hands clasped behind her back. The Presidents would be on board in a few minutes. Master Chief Warrant Officer Hectora Hale and Chief Warrant Officer Paris Larson. Kobayashi knew everything there was to know about them that hadn't been covered in black ink. Some of that too. She knew that they had been part of the covert unit that had bombed Edward's Spire, and that Larson was married to the pilot the Presidents flew with. She also knew that the Presidents wore the same armor as her Mithril team and that they had worn it for most of the war. She knew that meeting them would be difficult after all this time. And she could wait no longer.

Kobayashi left her quarters, striding down the stark white hallway. The lights went out for a moment, and she stopped. When they turned back on, she took a couple steps forward, then turned to return to her quarters. There were enough redundancies on ships of this caliber that the lights should never go out. Something was wrong. As she approached her quarters, she saw two of her marines, Silver and Smith, walking quickly. Both carried sidearms. Kobayashi's mind raced. No marine should be armed outside of established weapons training hours. They beat her to the door and stood in front of it.

"Sorry, major. We're not to allow you in."

"I'm your commanding officer. Move aside."

"There are orders higher than your chain of command."

Kobayashi didn't hesitate. Striking out with a flat hand, she smashed Silver's larynx. As Smith reached for his gun, she knocked it out of his hand and kneed him in the groin. He doubled over in pain while Silver held his throat, gasping. Kobayashi kicked one of the guns away and picked up the other. Smith was recovering from her strike. She took aim at his thigh and pulled the trigger. A flash and the smell of burning flesh and blood. Red splashed the white wall and pooled on the floor. Smith screamed and collapsed. Kobayashi turned to Silver and repeated the action. He fell to the ground as well.

Ignoring the continued wailing and rasping and the wet sensation she felt through her uniform Kobayashi moved to the wall. She pressed her hand against it, and it pulsed green. "Kobayashi to medical: Two injuries on Bravo Deck. Be advised, patients were hostile until subdued. It is unlikely that they will resist medical personnel." She pulled her hand off the wall and it pulsed blue, then green. With one glance at the two writhing men, Kobayashi scooped up the other gun and started off towards her officers' quarters.

When she arrived at the marine officers' bunk, she found Holtz and Allred playing cards at the table that sat between the two sets of bunks. There was no sign of trouble or of Goldman and Johansen. Holtz saw Kobayashi and started to get to his feet, frowning.

"Is there a problem, major?"

"Where's Johansen?"

"Hasn't been here all morning."

"Goldman?"

"Left right after that power flicker," Holtz answered. His eyes flicked down to the guns that Kobayashi carried. "What's going on, major?"

"Mutiny." She held one of the guns out to Holtz, handle first. Allred was on her feet now, eyes wide and shoulders tense. "Silver and Smith jumped me outside my quarters. I need you both to get to the barracks and get the marines organized. I don't know how many are in on this, but Johansen's the ringleader. Once you've got the men organized and armed, send a team to the bridge and sweep every deck. If you can talk any of the mutineers down, do it. Otherwise, you stop them using any means necessary, understood?"

"Yes, ma'am. What are you going to be doing?"

"I'm going after Johansen. There are two places this ship can be controlled from. I doubt she started with the main bridge."

"Won't you need back up?"

"I have a feeling I am the back up."

Clayton, Hale, and Larson were in the lift, headed down to E Deck when the lights went out a second time. The lift screeched as emergency protocols slowed it down and Clayton's stomach pushed upward. He thought he might throw up. Then the lift stopped, and the lights came back on. The lift continued but Clayton had his hackles up. Nothing like this should happen on any spacefaring ship, let alone a state-of-the-art ship like *Trafalgar*. And there was that security protocol hiccup on deck C earlier. Clayton glanced at Hale who looked even more agitated than she had coming off the *Grizzly*.

"Still working out the kinks in this new ship, captain?" Larson's voice was light and easy.

Clayton shook his head. "Haven't had any problems like this. Could be related to dropping out of the corridor but..." Clayton shrugged. He glanced at Larson who looked straight ahead at the door. His fingers tapped his side next to his firearm. Clayton looked up at the man's face and the door slid open. Larson drew his gun and Hale was a split second behind him, their helmets dropping to the ground. Then Clayton saw why. Two of Trafalgar's marines stood outside the elevator with weapons drawn on them.

"Did you ask for an escort, captain?" Larson edged in front of Clayton.

Clayton swallowed the lump that had formed in his throat. "No, I did not." He held his head up. Spadt! Clayton should have trusted his gut. He wondered who else was in on it. It couldn't be a NF plot, could it? Surely Dixon was trustworthy.

"Easy there," said the marine on the left. "There's some administrative reorganization in the works and we just need the captain to come with us. Put down your guns. No need for this to get messy." Larson chuckled. The sound sent a chill down Clayton's spine.

"I've spent the past month stewing on a shuttle, with nothing to do but wonder what happened to my friends who took a light-speed ride to God knows where. I'm itching for anything to break up the monotony, and this is looking like a ripe opportunity." The marine looked at his fellow mutineer. They both looked uncertain which gave Clayton a certain amount of courage.

"I don't have time for this," Hale said and before Clayton could respond, she fired her gun. Clayton instinctively raised an arm in front of his face and closed his eyes as bright light flashed, twice, three times. Heat flooded the elevator and screams erupted.

When he opened his eyes, the marines were on the ground, smoke rising from their chests. Blood was spattered all over the hallway and their bodies. The smell of charred flesh and metal permeated the air and again he felt like he might throw up. He swallowed the bile rising in his throat and looked at Larson.

Smoke rose from scorch marks on his chest plate which he rubbed at, frowning. "It's going to take a lot of scrubbing to get this off."

Ignoring the acrid smell that mixed in the air, Clayton forced himself to take a deep breath and stepped out of the elevator. One of the marines on the ground groaned weakly and raised a hand.

"We need to get these men to medbay."

Hale stepped out after Clayton. "I think you have more pressing concerns, captain. Someone is trying to seize control of your ship." She looked from one marine to the other. "Notify medbay if you like. Then we better get to the bridge and assess the situation." She bent and retrieved one of the guns and offered it to Clayton. Clayton hesitated for a second before taking the weapon. He had a basic proficiency with laser weapons, but they still made him uneasy.

Clayton palmed the wall. "Clayton to medbay. Two casualties on E deck Section L: Laser inflicted chest wounds. Use caution—patients may be dangerous." He took his hand off the wall and looked at Hale. "Alright. Let's go." Clayton glanced at Larson who had just fit his gold, egg-shaped helmet over his head and had Hale's blue one in hand. He tossed it to Hale, who put it on.

"I'll take point," Hale said. "Which way to the bridge?" Clayton pointed down the hall and she started off.

"After you, sir." Larson waved Clayton along and took up position in the rear. It wasn't far to the bridge. When Hale reached the door, she took a position by the side of the door while Larson came to stand in front of it. He gave her a nod and motioned for Clayton to stand up against the wall, behind Hale. He did so and Larson and Hale took up positions on either side of the door. Larson nodded at Clayton, and he pressed his hand against the wall. The door opened and Larson rushed in.

"Everyone stay right where you are!"

Hale followed him in, and Clayton strained his ears to hear what was happening inside. Raised voices, but no gunfire. Clayton shook his head. He couldn't do anything if he didn't know what was going on. He swung into the bridge to find Hale and Larson standing off against a fireteam of marines positioned around his chair where Spadt stood. Clayton recognized one. Sergeant Major Fegan. Kobayashi had served with him during the war. Was he in on the conspiracy?

"Captain Clayton, thank God you're alright." Spadt stepped forward, motioning for the marines to lower their weapons, which they did. Clayton lowered his own gun, taken aback. Was Spadt genuine? Or was this a feint?

"At ease, Hale, Larson." Clayton stepped forward as they lowered their weapons. "What's going on here, commander?"

"It's Johansen, sir, the marine spec-op commander. At least, that's what Kobayashi told her lieutenants. They sent Sergeant Major Fegan to secure and protect the bridge while they swept the ship for more mutineers."

"Johansen?" Clayton frowned. "Why would she want to take the ship over? And if she's not here, what's going on?" Then it dawned on him. The security blip, the flickering lights. It was beginning to come together. If someone was going to take over the ship, overriding command from the auxiliary bridge would be much easier and less dangerous than storming the main bridge.

Clayton looked at Fegan. "Take your team up to C Deck immediately. The auxiliary bridge. She'll be trying to override our command functions."

"Yes, sir. Let's go, boys." Fegan led his small team off the bridge and Spadt stepped to the side, opening his arm towards Clayton's chair.

"You have the bridge, sir."

Clayton nodded shortly and took his seat. He forced himself to take a deep breath. He looked down at the department heads below him, heart racing. He hadn't noticed it until now. Once he had composed himself sufficiently, he issued his first order. "Jones, Dixon, I want a sitrep and a report from Kobayashi and all her officers as soon as possible. Send runners if you can't get them on comms. And inform Admiral Villeneuve that we'll be delayed."

"Should we say why?"

Clayton frowned. "Yes, that would be prudent," he said, shaking his head.

"Aye, sir." They went to work on their assignment and Clayton put a hand to his chin, still frowning.

Why was Johansen of all people trying to take over his ship?

Kobayashi hurried along the corridor. No bulkheads slowed her down. Goldman must have taken care of them on his way to stop Johansen. She wasn't far now, and she thought she heard voices.

She slowed a little; there was no need to telegraph her presence. Goldman was alone but Kobayashi doubted Johansen was. Surprise reinforcements would be the best advantage he could hope for.

She was nearly at the door now. She heard Johansen's voice, loud, words indistinct. Then, one crisp, clear line from Goldman.

"Sounds like bullshit to me."

Kobayashi sped up. Light flashed from the open doorway. She swung in, registering two bodies falling. Johansen stood in her Mithril armor, gun raised, helmet off. She raised her weapon, trained it on Johansen's face and pulled the trigger. Johansen disappeared under the light of the laser and Kobayashi continued into the room, checking the corners. Empty. A quick glance at Johansen, covered in blood, her face melted told Kobayashi everything she needed to know. She rushed to Goldman's side. His body convulsed and he gasped and coughed.

She knelt by his side, looking at the black hole in his chest, oozing blood. She had seen wounds like this during the war. She knelt in front of him, blood seeping through her pants and put a hand on his shoulder.

"Why didn't you wait for me?"

"Couldn't risk it." Goldman's chest heaved. "A couple more minutes and she..." He coughed, the sound harsh. Deep. Blood speckled Kobayashi's uniform. His eyes stared off toward nowhere. "A couple more minutes, all she needed." Suddenly he locked eyes with her and dropped a heavy, unsteady hand on her shoulder. "Stay with me. Until—" He coughed hard again. "Until I'm gone."

Kobayashi grabbed his free hand and gripped it tight. "I'm not going anywhere, Jeff."

"Never..." He choked and coughed again, spraying another mist of red onto Kobayashi's uniform. "...really took you for a hand ... hand-holder." His hand slid down her shoulder, his eyes drifted away from her, and his head fell back. His grip in her hand went slack. Kobayashi sat up, pulling Goldman's body with her. She heaved a breath and closed her eyes, holding him to her body, cradling his head against her chest.

Clayton paced from one end of his office to the other, breathing deeply while he waited for the admiral's call, still processing the attempted mutiny. He didn't understand the motivation. The participants weren't divided on old corporate lines and none of them were talking. If it hadn't been for the loyal marines' swift action, Johansen would have been successful. Clayton owed Kobayashi his ship. Her, as well as Goldman. As grateful as he was, it shouldn't have been necessary.

Clayton's desk warbled and he strode over and gave it a tap. Villeneuve and Amin appeared, slightly blurred, as always. "Admiral. Captain." He nodded to them each in turn. Amin returned the nod, but Villeneuve skipped any pleasantries.

"How did this mutiny happen under your watch, Clayton?"

"No one saw it coming, admiral," Clayton said, locking eyes with Villeneuve. "None of the mutinous crew members were flagged as troublesome and whatever displeased them remains unclear; they aren't talking and we only have access to their dossiers. At this distance we're not connected to Zoar's Web. As it is, I've already ordered tighter security around the auxiliary bridge and my people are looking into the vulnerabilities Johansen was trying to exploit."

"Have you found any correlation between the mutineers?" Amin asked. Her tone was neutral, and Clayton was grateful for that.

"They seem to come primarily from rural districts, mostly in the northern latitudes of New America. Several, including Johansen, grew up in Ritty Communes before leaving that life behind."

"Ritties? Those nuts that think we should give up all technology after the plow?" Villeneuve scoffed. "That's hardly the kind of people to take over a spaceship."

Amin frowned. "There might be something to that, actually." Clayton frowned at her, but she continued. "Ritty comes from an initialism—RTE: Return to Earth."

"Of course," Clayton said, as realization hit him. "Ritty" had become a word all its own and people tended to forget where it came from. Including Clayton, it seemed. "Rejecting technology is only one part of their beliefs. Some more extreme members believe that living on Zoar is unnatural, that we don't just need to emulate the humans of earliest history but that we need to literally return to Earth."

"That's a contradiction in terms." But Villeneuve was frowning now himself. "How could you return to Earth without using highly advanced technology?"

"'Sometimes in order to create light, one must use tools discovered in darkness.' Greenacre's Genesis: Our Ark," Clayton quoted.

"Even with that, how would they get to Earth? No one knows where it is. Did they think they could just fly off into space and magically appear there?" Silence met Villeneuve's questions. Clayton didn't have an answer for them, not one he could support anyway, and it didn't seem Amin did either. Villeneuve sighed and shook his head. "Maybe that's exactly what they thought. Stupidity persists through every period of history, huh?" No one spoke for a moment. Then Villeneuve asked, "What about the Presidents? What happened with their debriefing?"

"They're understandably frustrated and on edge. We're still parsing through the extra data they brought in, but nothing has been forthcoming."

"And what are you doing with them now?"

"Given their skill set and desire to get in the action, I've assigned them to the marines. I'm sure Kobayashi will put them to good use."

Kobayashi woke up with a gasp, sweating. Taking a moment to gather herself, she steadied her breathing. She sat up and checked the time: 0432. She closed her eyes for one deep breath. Then, she swung her legs over the side and stood up. She stepped away from the bed and lowered herself into a push-up position. She did one, then another and continued until her breathing became labored and her body shook. Then she did one more.

Finally, she let herself down and lay on her back on the hard floor until her breathing steadied again. Then she rolled over and did another set. As she rested after that set, Kobayashi knew she shouldn't do another. She still had PT and drill with the platoon; she didn't need to tire herself out before that. She needed to show continued strength after what had happened the day before.

She rolled over and did another set.

When she arrived at the meeting point outside Cargo Bay F, she counted heads. All totaled, she was down fifteen soldiers, even with the Presidents and their pilot added in. She was going to have to consolidate the platoon; she didn't have the strength necessary for three squads. The defectors and those who died or were injured subduing them had come from each of them. Fortunately, she still had Holtz and Allred, as well as Fegan, who stepped in beside her. He glanced at her, looking to see if she was ready to start the morning run. She held a hand up and stepped forward.

"Thank you all for performing your duties yesterday. Our numbers are thin, but Captain Clayton has seen fit to supplement our forces with three naval personnel." Kobayashi gestured to Hale and Larson and their pilot, Anderson, all of whom stood apart from the others. "Lieutenant Anderson, Master Chief Warrant Officer Hale, and Chief Warrant Officer Larson. After PT today, I will confer with my officers about how we are going to reorganize the platoon." Kobayashi looked out at the marines' faces. Most of them met her gaze. A few looked down. She exhaled quietly.

"What happened yesterday was a betrayal of our trust. Those who tried to take over the ship did so with no regard for their brothers and sisters aboard. But now we know where each of us stands; there is no room for suspicion or anger at the man standing next to you. Given all this, now seems a fitting time to tell you the nature of our mission."

All eyes were on Kobayashi now.

"Almost two months ago, a research ship investigating a possible green planet was destroyed. Command suspects foul play. We are the second ship that has been sent to investigate. The first was manned by the Presidents, all of whom were abducted, with the exception of our new additions. Who or what took them we don't know. Our mission is to figure that out and retrieve the Presidents." Kobayashi looked over at Fegan and nodded. He returned the gesture and stepped forward.

"Now, get to running!"

"We need to combine what's left of Alpha and Bravo." Kobayashi stood in a conference room with her officers, as well as Fegan. In the stark white aesthetic, every face was expressionless. Most all arms were crossed. Only Fegan sat, his arms crossed on the table.

"Holtz, Anderson, I want you to lead the new squad." Kobayashi continued. "Technically, you have a higher rank and combat experience, Anderson, but since Holtz has greater tactical training, I'm putting him in overall command, while I take command of Mithril. Allred, you'll still be the XO for that squad. Hale and Larson are going into that squad as well. For the last couple spots, I think Sergeant Major Fegan and Private Hammond are the best candidates. Questions?"

"Yes, ma'am," Holtz asked. "Who's platoon XO?"

"You are," Kobayashi said, but she glanced at Allred. "At this point there is little to distinguish either of you, but with only two squads, it seems prudent that I command one and my XO commands the other."

"Understood, major."

Allred cleared her throat and Kobayashi looked at her. "Yes, lieutenant?"

"Oh, I uh," Allred said, shifting. "I was just thinking this is the part where Jeff would have said something about you just wanting some of the Mithril armor. Sorry, major. Stupid joke."

Kobayashi's mouth twitched. "That... is something he would have said."

Anderson grinned. "I wouldn't blame you, major. I hear it's comfy. I wouldn't want to give it up either." Allred's mouth tugged up at the corner.

A moment passed, then Kobayashi said, "Does anyone have any more questions or concerns?"

Fegan leaned into the table a bit. "I have one, major."

"Go ahead, sergeant major."

"Well, now that our general mission parameters are known by the whole platoon, is there anything more specific that those of us in the room now should know?"

Kobayashi glanced at Anderson and shook her head. "There are more detailed reports from Hale and Larson, but we're still in the dark about what kind of threat we're facing. I'll forward the reports, but don't expect to find answers there. I'm due to debrief Hale and Larson in greater depth than their report indicates. If anything new and relevant comes to light, I'll let you know."

"Understood, major."

Kobayashi looked from one side of the room to the other. No one offered any other questions and she nodded. "Right. You're all dismissed." All of the officers filed out of the room except Anderson who made herself comfortable, half-sitting on the table.

"So, Major Kobayashi ... Congratulations on the promotion."

Kobayashi raised an eyebrow. "What would you know about that?"

Anderson shrugged, smiling slightly. "I have a lot of free time as a pilot, so I read. Mostly technical manuals or history. Before we left Zoar, you were still a captain."

"And why were you keeping tabs on me?" Kobayashi crossed her arms.

Anderson's smile disappeared. "The same reason you split me up from Paris and Hectora. *She* doesn't recognize you, but Paris and I do. And it's a good thing for you it's not the other way around, major. Hectora doesn't let things go easily."

"It was war."

"She saved you!" Anderson stood up straight.

"One crisis of conscience after thousands of—"

"Careful, major," Anderson took a step towards Kobayashi. "Everyone's hands are bloody."

"I know," Kobayashi whispered. She dropped her arms to the side, eyes flicking from one side of the room to the other before meeting Anderson's stare. She crossed her arms again. Anderson didn't look angry. If anything, her expression was soft. Pitying. Kobayashi rolled out her shoulders. "You're dismissed, lieutenant."

"Aye, aye, major."

"I owe you an apology, commander." It had taken a couple days for Clayton to swallow a sufficient amount of his pride to call Spadt into his office. Now they stood in front of the desk and Spadt looked confused.

"An apology, sir?"

Clayton sighed and nodded. "You're an excellent officer. You've given me no reason to doubt you but when the mutiny started, my first thought was that you led it. For all my talk about needing to get over the war, I let it color my view of you. I'm sorry."

Spadt looked down. "Thank you, captain," he said looking back up. "After our conversation after launch…" He held an empty hand up. His mouth twitched and he dropped it.

Clayton nodded. "I won't doubt you again, Elias." Clayton extended a hand. Spadt shook it firmly. Clayton released Spadt's hand and walked around his desk. "A drink, commander?"

"Aye, sir."

Clayton retrieved the bottle of whiskey and two glasses. He filled them and offered one to Spadt. Raising his own, he offered a toast. "To trust."

Spadt clinked his glass to Clayton's. "To friendship out of adversity."

They drank.

"There is something you should know now," Clayton said, leaning back against his desk, glass set to the side. "Before she was destroyed, the *Erikson* was able to send back a preliminary report. There's evidence that Geneva might already have intelligent life."

Spadt cocked his head to the side. "What evidence?"

"Images of what appear to be clear cut forests, large geometric shapes that are consistent with what one would expect from farms or cities."

Spadt nodded slowly. "I see why you wanted to keep this quiet. It's enough to start speculation but not to confirm anything."

"That's what bothers me."

"Sir?"

Clayton stood from the desk, arms crossed. "Villeneuve shared that information and some of the imagery, but I get the feeling there's more evidence that he withheld. Not just a feeling—even a data packet compressed for transmission through relays would have had more than just a few images from orbit."

"Why would he withhold information?"

Clayton began pacing the room. "Did you study much history in school, commander?"

Spadt shook his head. "Only what was required, sir."

Clayton nodded thoughtfully. "I studied Earth history for my E.E. Focused on the European colonial period. Do you remember any of that from school?"

"Just that America was colonized then."

"Thing is, there were already people in America when it was colonized. All of the Americas, not just the United States. Those native populations were technologically inferior. The European powers subjugated, absorbed, or destroyed them. In areas they didn't conquer entirely, they still upset the existing societies and continually meddled in them. The suffering went on for generations. At the time of the Exodus, there were still a large portion of native descendants suffering from the consequences of European colonization hundreds of years before."

"And you're afraid that the same thing could happen to whatever intelligent life there might be on Geneva."

"Precisely." Clayton stopped and sat on the edge of his desk. "How long has it been since Humanity ran into a new culture?" He said. "Back on Earth they were all human and still the technologically superior conquered and molested the primitives they came into contact with. One could claim that we've matured as a race, but I'm not convinced, especially given how long it's been since anything like this has happened. And this could be a truly alien intelligence in every way, which makes the opportunity for conflict greater and the justification of domination more digestible."

"If that's the case, why would the Admiralty want to hide the possibility of intelligent life? Unless..." Spadt crossed his arms, frowning, and continued. "Unless they don't know what to expect from the public. They want to control the narrative."

Clayton nodded. "The more they know about the life there, the more they can distort that knowledge to their purposes. An ambiguous 'alien life' leaves too much to the imagination and, especially given the public opinion of the Admiralty after the war, I wonder if the Admiralty has even shared the information with Director Bear, although it's easy to imagine that he could be in on it."

"What are we going to do about it?"

Clayton shrugged. "For now, nothing. We don't have any more information to act on than the Admiralty. But when it comes down to it, if the Admiralty tries to convince the public that we have the right to conquer an intelligent world, can I count on you to stand beside me?"

"One hundred percent, captain."

Kobayashi stood next to her bed in her quarters, across from Hale and Larson. Larson sat in one of the chairs at the table while Hale lounged against the table itself.

"Walk me through your insertion on the alien ship. I have your report, but I want any details you might have left out."

"We know how a debriefing works, major," Hale said. Kobayashi inclined her head but said nothing. After a moment, Larson shrugged his shoulders and Hale sighed.

"There's not a lot more," she said. "We were the last pair out of the shuttle."

"What did it look like?"

"It was dark. Cramped," Larson said, gesturing to make a small box with his hands. "Corridors were only six and half feet high, four maybe five feet wide. Felt like I was going to smack my head with every step I took."

Kobayashi leaned forward slightly. "Did you see any sign of the ship's operators?"

"No." Hale shook her head, biting her lip.

"But?" Kobayashi caught Hale's eye, but Hale hesitated. Larson spoke instead.

"We've got a working theory, major. Nothing definite."

"Let's hear it." Kobayashi looked back at Larson. He was proving to be more cooperative. To her surprise, Hale spoke up.

"The ship was automated."

"What makes you think that?"

"Well," Larson said, "I know that if I had intruders on board, I'd sound an alert, try to get rid of them before leaving. The only reason I can see not to do that is if our presence wasn't detected or there was no protocol in place."

Hale continued Larson's thought. "There was no sign we were detected, but it's too much of a coincidence that the ship woke up and left the system so quickly after we came aboard."

"We think it returned to wherever it came from for further orders."

Kobayashi leaned back, arms crossed. "Any other reasons for that thought?"

"We had open comms with the rest of the Presidents right up until the ship jumped out," Hale said. "None of them reported seeing anything onboard the ship."

Kobayashi nodded. "A reasonable theory." She paused, then stood, hands clasped behind her back. "There's one other thing." She looked from Hale to Larson. "We all know that the chances of finding the Presidents are slim. Slimmer still is finding them alive. They've already been MIA for a month. Are you both ready to face that possibility?" Larson and Hale were silent for a few moments before Hale nodded firmly.

"Aye, ma'am."

"Aye."

Kobayashi nodded. "Good. You two are dismissed for the day. We have PT at 0700 tomorrow morning." Larson stood and he and Hale saluted and made their way for the door. Once they were gone, Kobayashi exhaled and straightened her uniform. It wasn't definite, but it was more than they'd had to go on before. She had to get fitted for her armor.

CHAPTER X

Throughout Meen,
Throughout Meen,
Throughout Meen the Narssarn traveled
In the hands of the crowned Keem.
—Traditional Meltish verse

It was two days before Fred learned the name of the village he and Shar'hre had been taken to: Liladee. Most of those days were spent with Ema'eln. She spoke with Shar'hre while Fred sat nearby and listened, doing his best to follow the back and forth. He could now differentiate words and follow the cadence of the language decently but his vocabulary and understanding of other nuances was still too limited for full comprehension.

On the morning of the third day, Ema'eln came to them while Shar'hre stretched on one side of the hut that they had been provided and Fred sat in the hammock. She carried a large bowl of groop, as they called it. It was typical *rektasd*, and while Fred had initially been put off by the fact that the culture often ate from the same bowl, he now appreciated it for what it was. As Ema'eln entered, Fred decided to take the initiative. Standing from the hammock he gave her a small bow.

"Sahdah, Shash."

"Sahdah, Fred." She returned the bow and turned to Shar'hre who had risen from her place on the floor. "Sahdah, Shar'hre."

"Sahdah, Shash Ema'eln. A'u chew?"

"Aym dalh. Ayhreshid dahl en ayil drongah." She took a seat on the floor and Fred and Shar'hre joined her, sitting cross legged. Ema'eln distributed the straws and said her usual prayer, which Fred was beginning to pick apart though he still lacked the necessary vocabulary. The groop that Ema'eln made was similar but distinct from Shar'hre's recipe. This was thicker and more textured. Still sweet but with a slightly bitter aftertaste. Fred wondered if it was a difference of recipe from village to village, hut to hut, or if there was a large selection of groop recipes that were widely prepared. Fred released the straw from his mouth when the sound of yelling reached him from outside. He looked at Ema'eln, then Shar'hre, as the shouts grew louder.

Ema'eln stopped drinking as well and looked him. "D'cheerhra ad?"

Fred nodded and saw Shar'hre's brow furrow as she heard it as well. She stood and walked to the door, Ema'eln and Fred close behind her. Fred saw a child running down the road towards them, and a couple men ran the other way, carrying spears. Then, Ema'eln pushed him back into the hut, speaking rapidly to Shar'hre who nodded vigorously. Then, Ema'eln rushed outside.

"What's going on?" Fred looked at Shar'hre, trying to figure out how to translate it. "Uhd pushandguin?"

"Hrintar."

Fred paced while Shar'hre stood by the doorway, looking into the street. As far as he could figure, it had been at least half an hour. Shar'hre had not been forthcoming with details and the village had grown quiet after Ema'eln left. Fred had been through a few raids during the war on Zoar. He had believed he could feel violence and fear in the air then and that feeling returned to him now. Whatever was going on involved death. Why would Hrintar be staging an attack on his grandmother? The only conclusion Fred could come to was that it had to do with the fact that Genit and Gal'Leah had kidnapped Shar'hre and him. Were they—was *he*—that important?

Fred stopped pacing and looked at Shar'hre, whose gaze didn't waver from the road outside. The idea of blood being spilt over him made Fred sick to his stomach. He'd actively protested the war on Zoar. He hadn't even had a stake in it. Here, however, he might be the reason people were fighting. That, or maybe the excuse. He put his hands on his knees and took a deep breath, staring at the ground as his stomach churned. There had to be more to it than him. After a moment, he heard running outside and looked up at Shar'hre. She stepped back from the doorway and Gal'Leah stepped inside, speaking urgently.

"Wusho. Wusho nauwah." Fred started forward and Shar'hre wrapped an arm around him. He didn't need help walking anymore, but the support felt natural at this point, and it reassured him as Gal'Leah continued to speak rapidly with an edge in her voice.

They exited the hut. Immediately outside, everything looked as it should. The sun was shining, huts sat along the road, their yellow and green roofs and walls glowing in its rays. Even the *wins* floated through the sky as they always did. The only thing missing were the villagers, bustling about their day. Once again, Fred was reminded of raids during the war, of stepping out bunkers to find empty streets.

He didn't have long to think on that as Gal'Leah led them west, out of the village. They took no time to look where they were going, rushing down the road that cut through the trees. It wasn't long before Fred felt the road steepen and Gal'Leah led them into the forest. Through the brush and contorted trees they went, never pausing. Fred's leg was finally feeling better, but at times he found himself running or Shar'hre dragged him as they followed Gal'Leah up the hill. He had no idea where they were going and the growth was so thick he was having a hard time believing that Gal'Leah herself knew.

Then, he looked up and she was gone. Alarm crept up his throat until he felt Shar'hre pull him right. He looked and watched her disappear as she pulled him into a dark crack in a giant boulder overgrown with some kind of blue moss. It wasn't long before it was too dark for Fred to see anything, but Shar'hre kept an arm around him as they made their way slowly deeper into the darkness. Fred's breathing had slowed since they'd entered the cave, but he became more and more aware of it every time he looked over his shoulder to see the sliver of light that was the entrance to the cave shrink. Eventually the light was nothing more than a pinprick, so small that Fred thought he might be imagining it. About this time, Fred could reach out with his free arm and touch the side of the cave. It was closing in. Fred wondered briefly what kind of creatures might live in caves here.

Fred and Shar'hre continued through the cave, letting the walls guide them for a few more minutes. Then, the walls fell away and Fred thought he saw a red glow in the distance. They made their way toward it. As they drew near, silhouettes of people began to take shape around the light. Evidently, they were not the first to be evacuated from the village. Coming closer still, Fred saw that they were mostly children. Or at least, that was what he guessed, based on the fact that only three or four of them were taller than him. Among these was Gal'Leah, who Shar'hre steered towards. Once they reached her, Shar'hre released Fred and spoke to Gal'Leah in a low voice. They were quiet enough that Fred's basic understanding of the language couldn't discern anything, so he turned to take in the rest of the group.

Now that he was in the full circle of light, he saw that there were three adults besides Gal'Leah. Two men and another woman, and they all looked to be in their prime. Looking around at the children, Fred was surprised at just how young they all were. He didn't think the oldest was even twelve. In a converse manner there were no elderly. He had seen a few people in the village who looked to be around Ema'eln's age, but none of them were here. He glanced at the adults who each held a spear and had axes strapped to their sides and it dawned on him.

This was a warrior culture. If the age of people in this cave were a representation of who was considered unfit or not of fighting age, then children were expected to fight by the time puberty hit and to continue fighting until they died. There was no aging out. Looking around again, Fred saw no cripples, which meant that even the injured weren't exempt or that non-fatal injuries or disabilities were rare.

The adults wore grim faces. They were big, even for these people. Shar'hre was taller than most of the women he saw and both Gal'Leah and the other woman were taller than her. Although the men were seated, Fred guessed they were nearly a foot taller than himself. From a purely physical standpoint they must be formidable fighters. So why were they here and not in battle? Fred's gaze gravitated back to the children.

They watched the adults with wide eyes, but whispered in each others' ears, giggling and smiling. They didn't seem afraid. He watched one boy, a toddler, tentatively approach one of the men who sat cross legged on the other side of the fire. He said something and the man smiled, holding out a hand. The boy placed his hand in the man's. The man lifted him up with that single hand, twisted it so the boy faced outward, then brought him down, into his lap. He then picked up his spear and laid it sideways across his lap, letting the toddler feel the weapon.

Fred realized then that not only were these formidable warriors, they might very well be the best in Liladee. The warm treatment this man gave the boy and the complete lack of fear the children had, despite being rushed out of their homes into a dark cave, told Fred that children were the priority here. It was probably a great honor and responsibility to be left in charge of the next generation when one's village was under attack. Oddly, the calmness of the children instilled in Fred a similar feeling. He took a seat, crossed his legs, and took a deep breath. Hopefully the fighting wouldn't last long.

Why?

Such was the question in Shar'hre's mind as she paced the edge of the fire light, eyes swiveling from the darkness towards the cave exit and Hred who sat by the fire. Why would Hrintar raid his grandmother's village? He could easily have come and asked for Shar'hre. She would have set it straight. There was no need to fight.

That thick skulled Genit! If only he had not been so blind as to take them by force. He should have listened to Ema'eln. None of this would have happened if he had. Shar'hre felt her shoulders rise and her chest swell with anger. She would go to the Keem after the fighting. The feud between Genit and the Tuluchur had gone on long enough; Uahrey would settle it.

But why? Why had Hrintar chosen violence before trying diplomacy? He was Tuluchur. He was charismatic and powerful. Shar'hre knew of his feud with Genit, had heard murmurs about disagreements with Ema'eln, but how poor must his relationship with his grandmother be to attack her village rather than speak with her?

Shar'hre paused in her pacing and looked around at the people around the fire. Gal'Leah, pregnant as she was, held a child in her lap, as did each of the other warriors. Hred sat, looking calm as he usually did. She knew he must understand the danger of the situation. He had certainly sensed the urgency while they fled to this cave and, when Genit (a man twice Hred's size) had raised his hand against her, he had thought to rise against him. She was glad he had thought better of it.

She wondered if Hred was always so calm. It was fitting for a Telahren, but he seemed ... resigned to that role. Did his calm come from acceptance of a lack of power instead of some kind of certainty? As many people had asked, what kind of messenger could not speak? What kind of messenger didn't know his message? Shar'hre shook her head. She shouldn't think like that. Always before she had trusted Hrintar. His teachings aligned with the beliefs Shar'hre had been raised with. They complemented and elevated her understanding of the world, both physical and spiritual.

She continued her pacing around the fire. Tuluchur or not, Hrintar was a man. Was it possible that even in his high station, he was susceptible to fault? Did his office protect him from that? If so, where was the line between Hrintar the man and Hrintar Tuluchur? Surely the Jeli'ahsh would not allow him to mislead followers in their faith. Shar'hre sighed and her eyes fell on Hred. She broke from her circular prowling and sat down next to him.

He looked at her. His brow furrowed and he leaned towards her, a hand extended. She placed her hand in his. The pressure as he squeezed it reassured Shar'hre. Without a thought, she leaned into him and rested her head on his shoulder.

There was a sound toward the entrance of the tunnel. Shar'hre squeezed Fred's hand and let go. Everyone in the cave stood. The warriors readied their weapons and themselves. The children scurried back behind them and Fred, unarmed and confident in his own incompetence, joined them though he placed himself in front of them. He wouldn't be much use as their defender, but he agreed with these people that children were more important. He looked at Shar'hre as she stood a step to the side of the rest of the warriors, her face hard.

The source of the noise came into view. Ema'eln stood tall and strong, a spear in hand. Fred saw that her brilliant white hair had dark splotches in it and after a moment he realized that it was drying blood. Her clothing shone with streaks of blood as well and her hands and arms were coated in it as well. As she drew near, the smell of iron washed over him.

Gal'Leah approached Ema'eln, an earnest question in her voice. Ema'eln lifted her chin and shifted her grip on her spear, so that when she made a fist around it, the blade was pointed down. Then, she drove it into the ground. Gal'Leah sighed audibly and hurried to the older woman, wrapping her arms around her.

Fred felt a hand on his shoulder and turned, unsurprised to see Shar'hre. She looked at him with lips downturned and a furrowed brow. Fred glanced around at the others and saw only smiles. He looked back at Shar'hre and nodded solemnly. Whatever victory Ema'eln and Genit had had over Hrintar, the root of the dispute had yet to be resolved.

CHAPTER XI

To the east
To the east
To the east the Narssarn departed
In the hands of explorers bold.
—Traditional Meltesh verse

Shar'hre walked alongside Ema'eln at the head of the column. Hred walked behind them, Genit beside him. A dozen of Genit's *hroan* accompanied them on the march to Gid'Del. They had left the morning after the raid. The wounded were taken care of, Hrintar's *hroan* as well as their own. The no'ihrah of Liladee was an older man and entirely competent. Four people had died before Hrintar had retreated. Fortunately, most of the wounds were not life threatening, and the no'ihrah had mostly attended to the wounded before Shar'hre had even returned from the cave.

Shar'hre did not like leaving the wounded so soon after, but they had all been in agreement; she must attend the *Muldun*. She must hear Hrintar's reasons and logic in light of Ema'eln and Genit's. She could not condemn the Tuluchur, though Genit had demanded it of her following the attack. At the same time, she could not stand for his feud with Genit and Ema'eln to bring more to harm. It must end, but she failed to see how. She would have to trust in Keem Uahrey's wisdom.

It was a long march to Gid'Del. They stopped only twice to rest and nourish themselves. Hred sat near Shar'hre during these breaks and though he said little to nothing, she was grateful for his calm presence. As they drew nearer, the trail became familiar. She recognized a bend in the road here and there and knew they were drawing near the mah Hrintar had provided for her after Hred's arrival. She smiled at the thought, though a tightness rose in her chest.

It was the ideal environment for a no'ihrah and dehihrah, but Shar'hre felt something beyond that normal connection with Hred while he coalesced. Was it merely because he was Telahren? She had never felt for him the kind of awe that overcame her with Hrintar. Perhaps that was because she had seen him in his weakness or because he was clearly not a god, but a man. A short one at that.

Nevertheless, she felt comfortable with him, closer to him than to Hrintar, even if the Tuluchur was her lee'inkah. She wondered if that would change as Hred mastered Meltish and, if it did, if they would drift apart or grow closer yet. What thoughts, feelings hid behind his calm eyes? In matters determinable by observation Shar'hre felt she knew him better than she had known any other person. In other ways, she recognized that she knew nothing of him. And yet, how much did those ways matter? Hred's actions and predominantly calm manner told her all she needed to know about his character.

Fred had thought the scenery had become more familiar in the past few minutes of walking. His suspicion was confirmed when they reached a bend in the path and the trees opened up to reveal the very hut where he'd spent most of his time since crashing on the planet. He smiled when he saw it. His time there with Shar'hre had been peaceful, nearly idyllic. If it weren't for his leg and—well, everything that had happened to bring them together—it would have been paradise.

His eyes drifted to the side, where the charred ground marked the place where Dorothy's pyre had been. His smile retreated at the sight. Cold guilt branched through his chest and Fred exhaled as he confronted it. Guilt. Not that she was dead, but that her death had been part of a series of events that found Fred happier than he had been in years.

Even before the war on Zoar, he'd been discontent. He enjoyed his studies in history and language, but found himself frustrated, even sickened by bloated Renovamen society and culture. He'd often thought that something drastic needed to happen. A plague or some other catastrophic event that would remind them of the world they lived in, something that would cull the excess. Short of that he thought maybe it would be best if he just went and joined a Ritty compound. When he'd finally got away from it all, it was everything he wanted. But others had paid the price. The entire crew of the *Erikson* was dead. It wasn't his fault and he knew that. But he'd asked for it, if indirectly. And now he had to wonder if perhaps those who had died in the skirmish yesterday had paid that price for him as well. Hred sighed and closed his eyes for a moment longer.

He opened them as the group slowed as they drew near the hut. Ema'eln spoke with Shar'hre and Genit. Fred was able to glean that they had decided to stop but wasn't able to determine the specific details. Much like the conference they'd had the night before they'd left, Fred found that he got the gist, but not the whole deal. The party split up, some sitting down on the bare ground, others milling about and chatting. Shar'hre approached Fred, her face drawn together in concern.

"Archuh hray'id?"

Fred's eyes flicked to the charred spot of ground, but when he looked back at Shar'hre he nodded. "Aym hray'id."

She put a hand on his shoulder and looked into his eyes for a moment, before nodding. "Gum, Wushaheed."

Fred nodded and they put their arms around each other as they had grown so accustomed to and entered the hut.

The sun was touching the tree line as they walked into Gid'Del. People, many returning to their homes for the day, stopped and watched the procession. It was not uncommon for a group of that size to arrive in Gid'Del, but the people who made it up were unusual. Ema'eln, *eahro* of all Meen, she who turned back the Hrar'icohrean invasion, accompanied by Genit, enemy of the Tuluchur, Shar'hre, the Tuluchur's lee'inkah, and Hred Telahren.

No one stopped them as they made their way to the Keem's *Kual* and soon they reached the door. Genit, who walked next to Ema'eln at the front, held the flap open and she entered. Shar'hre and Hred walked side by side, just behind Ema'eln. When they reached the flap, Shar'hre stopped and took a deep breath. Hred put his hand on her shoulder, and she looked at him. They shared a small smile and moved inside.

The hall was large; often it was used as a communal gathering place. The whole shelter was a large, empty rectangular space. At the far end a two-foot-high dais ran the width of the wall. Three woven thrones stood upon it. In the center sat Keem Uahrey. To his right, the Princess Farloa and to his left Shash Kihrem, his sister. Standing behind the Keem was his *dahbahn* and standing on the dais to Kihrem's side, facing Uahrey was Hrintar. Shar'hre's heart sped up when she saw him.

Ema'eln led the group to the dais and stopped. Hrintar turned to face them and Uahrey contemplated them for a few moments before standing. Shar'hre felt Hrintar's eyes boring into her and she avoided his gaze. Her chest was tight. Her emotions crashed against each other like waves under distant moons.

Uahrey's eyes swept over the group before returning to Ema'eln. "I expected you would come, Shash."

"Hrintar has gone too far this time, Keem Uahrey. I invoke the right of *Muldun*."

Shar'hre risked a glance at Hrintar, but his gaze had not left her, and she looked away quickly, swallowing hard.

"This too I expected," Uahrey said. "Very well. The Tuluchur anticipated a Muldun and is prepared. We may begin now. Who first will speak against him?"

"I will," Genit said as he moved to the front of the group. Hrintar finally looked away from Shar'hre as he turned to face Genit.

They stood in front of the Keem and stared each other down: Genit, dark haired and massive; Hrintar red bearded, did not exceed his cousin in stature, but stood just as strong, arms crossed.

"You may begin, Genit Tygreen, son of Balatiy Tygreen and Ahruher," Uahrey said, settling in his chair. Genit squared his shoulders, and held a wide stance, as if ready to fight at a moment's notice. The tension in the room was thick. Shar'hre had attended only a few Muldun before and none had filled the room like this.

"Since my birth, I was promised the inheritance of my grandfather, Ahrul, *Ay Caitan* of Gahrither—the sword of Gahrither, with the Narssarn set in its pommel. Hrintar stole that birthright from me, claiming visions and guidance from the Ancestors. Furthermore, he professes to be the reborn soul of the man who slew my grandfather, his own brother Athorner. What reason is there in such a treacherous soul inheriting such a symbol?"

"That is the question you pose, Genit?" Uahrey asked.

"It is."

"My cousin asks rightly," Hrintar said, smiling thinly, voice quiet yet commanding. Shar'hre suppressed a shiver as he continued. "What right does the soul of treachery, murder even, have to the inheritance of he who was murdered? What right to even a body? Indeed, what right except that of redemption? I was reborn precisely to clean my blood from that inheritance." Hrintar bowed his head to Uahrey who nodded in return.

"Your question has been answered, Genit. Is there another who would speak against the Tuluchur?"

Ema'eln stepped forward. "I would." Genit descended from the dais, and she stepped up past him, stiffly. Genit stepped past Shar'hre and she could feel the heat of his breath as he passed. Ema'eln took her place across from Hrintar. She was the very image of regality, of strength and dignity, even with her silver hair stained dark in places. Hrintar no longer smiled and Uahrey continued the ritual.

"You may begin, Shash Ema'eln Tygreen, *Eahro* of the Belnor, daughter of Kalinte Tygreen and Alantor."

Ema'eln shook her loose hair away from her face. "From his youth, I raised Hrintar. He has made it no secret that he resents me for the absence of his parents following the Raricorean invasion. I held the Sword of Garither for Arul's daughter and when she denied it, I held it for her son. For this also, Hrintar resents me, for he has always coveted it. I raised him in the traditions of my people, which he forsook for Meltesh beliefs, and we grew further apart. I have the utmost respect for the beliefs of this land which took me in, but your Tuluchur has had naught but spite for me. Must the Meltesh suffer for our dispute?"

"Is this your question, Shash?"

"It is."

Hrintar was silent for a moment. "My grandmother believes that I resent her. I cannot deny that we have never shared a warmth like that which exists between her and my cousin. Anger often frustrated attempts to bond, but she is wrong to contend that our failure as a family resulted in the fighting at Liladee. If it were not for Genit's active attacks on my character and attempts to usurp that which the Jeli'ahsh revealed and consecrated to my purpose as Tuluchur, there would never have been conflict. In an attempt to reclaim the inheritance his mother forfeited, he carried away the Telahren and my lee'inkah. It was in their defense that I led my followers to Liladee. And there it was that Genit raised his hand in anger."

"I did no such thing!" Genit roared, stepping forward. Uahrey sprang to his feet.

"Silence!" Uahrey glared at Genit, who stopped in his tracks. "You have asked your question. Afford the *galnahn* the rights of the *Muldun*." Genit glowered for a moment but stepped back. Uahrey watched him for a moment before turning his gaze to Hrintar. "Continue, Tuluchur."

"I have answered the question, Keem," Hrintar said.

"Very well." Uahrey nodded to Ema'eln who moved to lower herself from the platform. One of the warriors who had accompanied them from Liladee moved to offer his hand, which she took and stepped down.

"Is there another who would speak against Hrintar Tuluchur?"

Shar'hre swallowed and stepped forward, heart thumping quickly in her chest.

"I would."

CHAPTER XII

I do not suggest that shared experience is invalid, but rather that alone the reinforcement of one's own experience and opinions is dangerous. It creates emotional and intellectual rigidity. What is rigid can only survive so much damage. The tree is sculpted by the wind until it can do nothing but uproot itself and fall in the next gust, quite possibly bringing down its neighbor.

—From "Why Now?" by Tobin Gorokhov

As *Trafalgar* approached the Schweiz System, Clayton exited his office into the familiar buzz of a bridge preparing to drop out of a FTL corridor. Members of the navigation department bustled around their pod of auxiliary workstations behind the main bridge, comparing calculations. Clayton made his way to his chair. Below the captain's chair, Castaño manned the flight console. Commander Dixon, sat to Castaño's left and Lieutenant Jones monitored the tactical situation at his station above them.

Clayton settled into his chair, sitting up straight. "Lieutenant Castaño, what's our status?"

"Final calculations are complete, Captain. Dropping out in ten."

"Good. You have control. Lieutenant Jones, I need readings the moment we drop out. We don't know what's out there."

"Aye, sir."

"Dropping out in 3, 2, 1."

Clayton leaned forward, holding his armrests. There was a mild jolt and Clayton released the armrests, impressed. "Dixon, Jones, status."

"All systems green, sir."

"Preliminary scans show us clear. Still waiting on long range."

Clayton nodded. "Keep an eye on it. Let me know at the first sign of trouble or when the *Nile* comes through. Alright, Castaño, move us toward Geneva, half ahead."

"Aye, sir, Geneva at half ahead." As Castaño set about the controls, Clayton stood and descended the ladder to stand to Castaño's right. Resting his hand on the top of Castaño's chair, gazing out into space. The system's sun, Schweiz, was center-right of their field of vision, large and yellow. Clayton strained his eyes to make out Geneva, but it wasn't readily visible yet.

"Can you see it yet, lieutenant?"

"Yes, sir. Eleven o'clock." Castaño pointed and tapped a couple controls. Four blue lines, two vertical and two horizontal, sprang from the bottom and the right, swinging to intersect around a white light that was significantly larger than the others in view, right where Castaño was pointing.

"Good eye, lieutenant. ETA?"

"Thirty minutes until we intersect the exterior moon's orbit."

"Alright. Just be sure to begin the deceleration before we're in atmo." Clayton smiled and clapped Castaño on the shoulder and climbed back up to the main level, then took the single step to his chair.

"ETA on the *Nile*, Jones?"

"Two minutes out, sir."

Clayton settled into his chair. "No anomalous readings?"

"No, sir."

"Let's hope it stays that way." Clayton tapped his right armrest twice. It lit up yellow and he spoke aloud. "Clayton to Commander Spadt and Doctors Cohen and Thao. Please report to the bridge." Clayton leaned back and kicked a leg up and glanced around the bridge. Things had calmed down a great deal. The crew in the three occupied auxiliary pods behind him had settled down, though there was still chatter as they went about less urgent work. Each pod consisted of four stations facing each other. Typically, these were filled with a junior officer belonging to the particular department and three enlisted crewmen. This team crunched numbers and parsed data for their immediate superiors at the main stations forward. The setup reminded Clayton of gun crews on naval ships in the golden age of the British Empire, though the physical division between the officers and their subordinates was different and had to be less efficient. Leave to engineers who had never set foot on a ship to design it.

Clayton heard the whir of the door to the bridge opening and Spadt walked through, followed by Cohen and Thao. He smiled and nodded to them. "We've arrived in the system. Commander Spadt, if you'd take the Mission station. Chiefs, take command of your mission pods. I think we're about to have a lot of information you'll find interesting." Clayton gestured to the singular empty group of consoles behind him. He hadn't had much need to interact directly with the doys—that is, members of the DOI—during this voyage and as a result, he hardly knew them. He made a mental note to spend more time with them in the future. "We'll be coming up on Geneva in about half an hour."

As the three new arrivals settled into their seats, Jones said, "Captain, the *Nile* has just dropped out of the corridor."

Clayton nodded. "Thank you, Jones. Commander Dixon, open a channel to the *Nile*."

"Aye, sir. Connecting now."

A moment passed before Amin's face appeared on the interior forward wall of the ship and her voice rang throughout the bridge. "Captain Clayton. I take it everything is under control?"

"No sign of the unidentified spaceship, captain. We're on a heading to Geneva now."

"Understood. We'll hang back until the *Tovey* arrives."

"Affirmative. We'll call if we need help."

"Likewise. *Nile* out."

The line cut and Clayton looked down at the flight station "Alright, Castaño, no need to hold back now. Full ahead."

"Aye, sir, full ahead."

"How much sooner will we get there, lieutenant?" Spadt asked. Clayton was glad his XO had the presence and the initiative to ask. He was still kicking himself for doubting the man in the first place.

"We should arrive at the outer moon in fifteen minutes, commander."

"Captain." Dixon looked back and up from her seat next to Castaño. "I'm picking up a distress signal. Standard Joint Fleet frequency. It seems to be coming from Geneva."

Survivors. Clayton hadn't allowed himself to hope, given the evidence the Presidents had brought back. "Hold onto that signal, Dixon. Castaño, compensate so we don't lose it with the planet's rotation." Clayton looked to Spadt. "Commander, forward a brief statement to Major Kobayashi. Have her scramble Mithril for a rescue op." Clayton was met with affirmatives from his officers, and he returned his gaze to the front where Geneva was growing larger and lighter, but still wasn't quite big enough to make out any details.

Cohen's voice sounded behind him. "Captain, if you're sending a team down, it would be prudent to inform them that gravity down there is one hundred and fifteen percent what it is back on Zoar. For every one hundred pounds they'll be carrying an extra fifteen."

Clayton nodded at Spadt. "Make sure they're aware, commander."

"Aye, sir."

Clayton stood from his chair and descended the ladder to stand next to Castaño. To the left, Geneva was growing larger and beginning to have its surface change from white light to green and blue. "There she is."

"Aye, sir."

"Doctors Thao and Cohen, would you care to join us down here? I think it's going to be quite the sight." Clayton glanced back briefly before returning his gaze to space. He heard the ladder clanging as the doys descended. Ahead, he was able to begin to pick out clouds and continents. It reminded him of Zoar and pictures and models he'd seen of Old Terra. Not Earth at its end but Earth in its prime—a blue globe, mottled with green and golden brown, swirled with white. A living world. They drew closer and one continent filled the screen. Center left of the planet were a pair of islands. The larger one was organically rectangular: four sides, the parallels of similar length. The other was a shapeless blot, almost entirely green with some kind of growth.

Clayton stirred from the view as Dixon spoke. "The signal is coming from the western part of the continent. That island, I think." She pointed and Clayton nodded.

"Put us in orbit, Castaño. Make sure we don't lose contact."

As Clayton turned to return up the ladder to his seat, Thao caught his eye. "It's marvelous, isn't it, captain?"

Clayton nodded. "I never thought I'd see another planet so much like Zoar with my own eyes." He turned to look at the planet again. The larger island was beginning to take up more of the view. He could pick out a large desert and maybe even a couple of mountain ranges among the green fields or forests. Were there really survivors from the *Erikson* down there? Were they alive, or had *Trafalgar* come too late?

Kobayashi marshalled Mithril outside the *Coon* class shuttle that the hangar techs were putting through pre-flight. Most of the team stood around in a loose circle talking, all in their white armor, with the exception of Hale and Larson, whose armor was blue and gold. Kobayashi's own armor rested heavy on her body but in a natural, well distributed way. The techs had done an excellent job of fitting it to her. She wasn't going to win any races, but it wouldn't impede her ability to do her job. The sound of boots on the *Coon*'s ramp told Kobayashi that Allred was joining them from the cockpit. She came to stand next to Kobayashi.

"Just about ready, major."

Kobayashi nodded. "Good." She raised her voice slightly. "Alright, people, gather in." The low murmur died down and the team drew closer. "We've picked up a distress signal from the surface of the planet. Our job is to go down and investigate and rescue any survivors. We have no information on what might be down there, but the planetologists have confirmed that the atmosphere will support life. Any questions?"

One of the rookies, Hammond, raised a hand. "Why didn't the Presidents pick this signal up?"

"We're not sure," Kobayashi said, "Working theory is that the *Grizzly* didn't get close enough to the planet to pick up the signal or that the planet was facing the wrong way when they arrived."

"Did the planetologists say anything about what the climate was going to be like?" Larson asked.

"Semi-tropical. The signal's coming from on an island in the mid northern latitudes. It could be wet or muggy. It's also going to be dark by the time we set down."

"Great," said Holland. "First time on an alien planet and we won't be able to see anything."

"We've got more important things to worry about, specialist," Fegan growled. Holland didn't respond and the group was quiet for a moment.

"Any more questions?" Kobayashi looked from one side of the circle to the other. No one said anything. A few heads shook. "Then let's load up." Kobayashi turned and led the team into the shuttle.

CHAPTER XIII

From the east
From the east
From the east Narssarn returned
In the hands of a warrior strong.
—Traditional Meltesh verse

The hall was dead silent as Shar'hre stepped forward. Fred had not understood everything that had been said, but it was clear that Hrintar was on trial. A trial unlike any Fred had witnessed before, but one that seemed infused with dignity and honor, a sharp contrast with the lawyering back amongst the Renovamen. He didn't fully understand the relationship Shar'hre had with Hrintar, but this unprecedented silence in the *Muldun* spoke volumes.

Shar'hre stepped onto the dais and took her place opposite Hrintar. Fred watched in anxious anticipation. Hrintar didn't look away from Shar'hre, but she didn't meet his gaze at first. She looked down, wringing her fingers. Then Uahrey spoke.

"Chewcapeguin, No'ihrah Shar'hre, Lee'inkah uf Hrintar Tuluchur, dahdlah uf Fohruthi en Shahnd." Swallowing, she nodded. She pressed her hands against her sides and looked up at Hrintar. A pit formed in Fred's stomach, and he did his best to clear his mind. Whatever was coming, he didn't want to miss it. If he couldn't decipher the meaning immediately, he had to remember the words.

"Ay ayvapin no'ihrah for only a few changes of the Greater Moon, but in that time, I have aided the elderly in their passing, the young in their foolish injuries, women in childbearing, even the Telahren in his convalescence. I was honored when Hrintar Tuluchur asked me to serve him, even more so when he took me as his lee'inkah. I have followed him faithfully ever since I first heard his teachings.

"But I am disturbed by the pattern I see in the life of Athorner and that of Athorner Reborn to Atone. The history, as you yourself have taught it, Hrintar Tuluchur, is that Athorner's sin was malice against his country and family. I ask this: what is the raid on your grandmother's village if not a beginning of the same sin? Will you continue the pattern or—" She stopped at the sound of shouting outside. An adolescent boy burst into the hall and ran to the front of the room.

"Keem Uahrey! Keem Uahrey!" The boy was out of breath as Uahrey rose to his feet. The boy took a couple of deep breaths and managed a single word, one that Fred did not recognize, but brought everyone's hackles up.

"Hrelhriansh."

Shar'hre dropped from the dais immediately, vaguely aware of the warriors around her drawing their blades or hefting their spears. She hurried to Hred's side as people flooded by them moving toward the door. Hred's face was drawn together in confusion, perhaps fear. She grabbed his hand and pulled him along with her, moving toward the doorway.

"We need to go." They were both unarmed and if a Hrelhrian raiding party was approaching Gid'Del... She couldn't allow Hred to come to harm. He was the Telahren. He was her friend.

He went with her readily. "Lesh." They drew near the door, but a voice stopped Shar'hre in her steps.

"No'ihrah!" She turned and saw Galeen, Uahrey's raven-haired dahbahn, approaching, carrying two spears. She offered Shar'hre one. "Here. The Keem wants you to take the Telahren somewhere safe, off the main road. Is there a place?"

Shar'hre took the spear, thinking a moment, then nodded. "Yes. Where his vessel crashed. The Hrelhrians will not know that place."

Galeen bowed slightly. "We will collect you after the fighting is over. Move quickly, No'ihrah. Bright blade."

"Swift blade." Shar'hre said, returning the bow. Galeen hurried away and, still holding hands, Shar'hre and Hred exited the hall. It was dark now and all down the road people bustled, preparing for the assault. It had been a long time since Hrelhrian had dared attack so deeply into Meen. Shar'hre had been a child at the time, but she remembered the aftermath. Not since the Hrar'icorhrean Invasion had a conflict within Meen taken half so many lives. Hrintar's feud with Genit did indeed seem petty in the face of the coming battle.

Shar'hre pulled her thoughts away from that and oriented herself. The vessel—where was it in relation to Gid'Del? Out, south and toward the river. She remembered a tree that marked where to go off the path, but it was outside the village, towards Hrelhrian. They would have to hurry. She pushed through the crowd, holding firmly to Hred's hand. She must not lose him. As they reached the edge of town, the crowd thinned. Once it was clear enough, Shar'hre broke into a trot and Hred went with her. She continued to speed up, watching the tree line for her landmark, until Hred yanked on her hand and they stumbled to a stop. Shar'hre turned to Hred, ready to scold him but saw his finger pointing straight ahead. She followed it and saw the glow of torches.

She cursed quietly and pulled Hred with her off the path into the woods. They made it only fifteen feet or so into the brush before a hair raising whoop sounded. Shar'hre turned to see the war party on the road, parallel with them as a cacophony of whoops answered the first. Shar'hre took a deep breath and clenched her hands. Hred squeezed back and she looked over at him. She had not meant to squeeze so hard, but she appreciated the reciprocation. It more reassuring than she might have expected. They would be fine. The war party had not seen them. Shar'hre watched until they were out of sight. The sound of their whooping faded as did the light from their torches, but Shar'hre didn't dare return to the road.

"Let us go," she said to Hred and they started out parallel to the road. It was still darkening. Shar'hre worried that she would not be able to find the landmark tree but after a few more steps there it was to the right with its trunk so gnarled that it nearly curled all the way around itself. Hred's vessel would be only a short way ahead and deeper into the forest. Not far now. She squeezed Hred's hand again, purposefully this time, and readjusted her grip on her spear.

They came from nowhere. If it weren't for the blood-curdling screech that preceded the attack, Fred would have had no warning. As it was, Shar'hre let go of his hand and something knocked him down. He scrambled to his feet, eyes darting around the dark forest, trying to follow the movements of the figures as his heart threatened to beat right out of his chest. How many there were, Fred couldn't tell for sure as they circled. Three, maybe four.

Shar'hre stood with her back to Fred, matching the movement of their assailants, spear held ready. One darted forward and she stepped back and to the side. The assailant retreated and another pushed forward, stabbing and Fred's heart leaped in his throat. He took a step forward, too late to help. Shar'hre had already stepped to the side, knocked the spear aside with her free arm and stabbed with her own.

Fred couldn't tell what happened next, but the man dropped his spear and fell back. Shar'hre had lost her spear and two more shadows jumped at her. She peddled backwards but couldn't get away from them. With a roar, Fred lunged forward and tackled the nearer shadow. They tumbled to the ground together. The moment they hit the ground, the man took control, rolling to pin Fred. He sat up on Fred's chest and reached to the side for something. Fred struggled to shove him off, but the man was much bigger than he was. The man found what he was looking for and brought the spear's point over his head. Fred's eyes widened and he slammed a hand as hard as he could into the man. Whatever he hit did the job. The man groaned and leaned to the side, just off balance enough that Fred was able to unseat him and roll away.

He got onto his hands and knees, but the man had already recovered. With a yell he stabbed at Fred who looked up to see the shadow of the spear coming down on him. A high-pitched scream interrupted the man, and a dark shape knocked the spear to the side. Fred could just make out Shar'hre's profile as she grabbed hold of the man. There was a grunt and a gasp, and the man doubled over, took a couple tottering steps, and fell to the ground.

Fred stood the rest of the way up. Shar'hre had a hand on her waist and her head turned, searching. Fred pushed down the impulse to hug her and checked their surroundings as well. Seeing no sign of movement, he approached Shar'hre.

"Are you okay?" Fred reached up and touched Shar'hre's face, then her shoulder. She put her own hand on his shoulder, looking up. She held up her hand and Fred looked down, the smell of iron reaching his nose. He touched her hand, which was warm and wet. His eyes widened. Shar'hre grabbed his hand and pressed it against her gut, which was hot and wet and pulsing. Bile rose in Fred's throat, and he swallowed.

"Ah, shit. No, no no." He tried to pull his hand away, but Shar'hre held it in place, meeting his eye. Panic swelled in his chest, rising into his throat with the bile. He tried to fight it off. "Right. You're right—pressure. Pressure." His mind was racing. What could he do? There were no doctors nearby, no first aid kits, nothing!

"Hred."

He looked at her, before looking straight down at the ground. "Hred, look at me." Fred looked back at her. Her eyes were slits, her mouth a thin line. "It is alright, Hred. It is not so bad." She touched his face, her hand wet with blood and his panic retreated a bit. Then she pointed behind him. "You see that tree there that curves left, then right, then curls? Big leaves?" Fred looked back. Which tree? There were a lot. It was dark. He took a deep breath and forced himself to scan more carefully. There! Broad leaves draped around it. He looked back at Shar'hre and nodded. "Go pull one of the leaves off. It will do until we can get to a no'ihrah." She slipped her hand under the one he held against her body. "Go. I have it."

Fred nodded and turned, running to the tree as quickly as he could. Fortunately, the tree was short, and he could reach up and snap one of the large bay-like leaves off with ease. It was almost as long as he was tall. He dragged it back to Shar'hre, who had sunk to a sitting position, leaning against a tree. She held a knife and nodded at him, looking down at the hand that was on her wound. He nodded and knelt down to replace her hand with both of his own. Shar'hre then pulled the bay leaf toward her. She cut off the stem and set the leaf in front of her, pinning it under a leg. She pulled her knife down the center of the leaf, cutting it into two strips. She then pushed herself back up to standing position, using the tree as leverage.

She looked at Fred. "Now, wrap these around *wesha*, tight, one on top of the other, this side up on the first one, down on the second one." She indicated the bottom part of the leaf, which was rougher than the other side. Fred nodded, let go of her side and got to work. The strips went around her waist twice each. Shar'hre held the first one tight where it ended, but when Fred wrapped the second piece around, the rough sides of both pieces stuck to each other. As long as Shar'hre didn't shift too much, the wrap would stay tight. Her breathing was loud and labored. Fred's chest tightened at its rasp, and he grimaced.

Draping Shar'hre's arm over his shoulder, he wrapped his own around her waist. "Alright, what now?" He looked at Shar'hre, but she could barely keep her head up. Indistinct shouting came from somewhere in the forest. Fred closed his eyes and took a deep breath. He had to get Shar'hre somewhere safe.

CHAPTER XIV

Historically this rigidity is a common cause of civil wars and revolutions. There are often other factors that are outside the control of either party, but failure to compromise is always an element of conflict as it necessarily escalates emotion, if not action.
—*From "Why Now?" by Tobin Gorokhov*

Clayton sat on the edge of his seat, waiting for word from Mithril. It had been nearly an hour since they'd been dispatched, and Clayton had nothing to do but wait and try not to look anxious. *Nile* and *Tovey* had taken their respective positions: *Tovey* in a parallel but more southerly orbit of Geneva; *Nile* around the outer moon.

"Captain Clayton." Clayton turned around to look at Thao, who sat in the mission pod with Cohen, frowning. "I've been studying the imagery of the main continent and there's something odd going on down there."

"Oh?" Clayton stood and walked back to stand behind Thao's console.

"Yes, look here. You see these patches?" He pointed at a few patches of grey. "At first, I thought they were exposed granite batholiths, but they're too random and geometric. Some occur in the middle of plains, well away from mountain ranges. And that's not all." Here he pointed to a different section of the picture, where a rectangular patch of yellow interrupted a sea of green. "I've determined that a lot of foliage down there is blue and yellow, but it's still mostly green. These patches of yellow? They're all very geometric as well. I don't think—"

"Sir, I'm getting a hail from *Tovey*." Clayton was relieved by the interruption. While he didn't want to keep his people in the dark, he wasn't ready to tackle the possibility of intelligent life on

Geneva just yet. He'd rather wait until Mithril returned from the surface and the immediate crisis was resolved.

"We'll continue this later, doctor." He moved to stand behind his chair in the center of the bridge. "Put it through, commander."

Villeneuve's voice emanated through the bridge. "Captain Clayton, Amin's picked up two ruptures on the edge of the system. It seems that the aliens brought reinforcements too."

"Aye, sir. What's their heading?"

"They're on a direct course for Geneva. I want you to move to assist Captain Amin."

Clayton looked at Castaño, nodding sharply. "Aye, sir. I've got my Flight department calculating the best trajectory right now."

"Good. Keep me apprised. Villeneuve out."

Clayton settled into his seat. "Castaño, I want to trail the outer moon's orbit by two hundred thousand kilometers."

"Aye, sir."

"Inform the *Nile* of our intent, Commander Dixon," Spadt said. Clayton was again grateful for the assistance in delegating the obvious. Clayton turned his attention to the tactical station.

"Lieutenant Jones, I want tactical analyses of those vessels ASAP. All crew on standby with all ordnance teams at the ready."

"On it, sir."

Clayton swiveled his chair to look back at the scientists. "Doctors, if you'd like to leave the bridge, now would be the time." Thao nodded and made for the door to the rest of the ship, but Cohen remained where she was.

"I'd like to observe, if you don't mind, captain."

Clayton nodded and swiveled to face the front again. "Of course, doctor."

"Captain, we're receiving a transmission from the *Nile*."

"Put it through, lieutenant."

Amin's voice emanated around the bridge and Clayton looked to the screen mounted on the left side where her face was displayed. "Captain Clayton, I'm going to attempt peaceful contact. I thought you'd want to hear."

"Of course, captain. Lead on. We'll follow your lead." Clayton looked into the dark void from which the alien vessels were coming. He doubted Amin would get through, but he would have done the same. Amin turned and faced forward and Clayton did the same on his ship two hundred thousand kilometers away. Then, she spoke in a clear, strong voice.

"Unidentified vessel, this is the Joint Renovamen Exploratory Fleet Ship *Nile*. We are here on a rescue mission and have no desire for conflict. Please respond."

Silence filled the bridges of both ships. Then Clayton heard Amin's tactical officer speak. "Ma'am, the lead ship is changing trajectory. It's now on an intercept course with *Trafalgar*."

"And the rear ship?"

"Still headed towards us."

Clayton spoke to the screen on the left. "I'll lead this ship off, Captain Amin." He turned to address his operations officer. "Commander Dixon, signal the admiral to fill the gap and support whichever of us needs it the most once the engagement begins."

"Captain Clayton." Clayton looked back to the screen, meeting Amin's eyes. "Good luck," she said.

"Likewise, captain. Clayton out." The screen went dark, and Clayton settled into his chair.

"Castaño, pull us away from the *Nile*, slowly. If the alien ship doesn't continue to adjust for us, stop moving away and inform me. Jones, analysis of the enemy ship."

Castaño indicated acknowledgement of his orders as Jones gave his report. "Titanium and aluminum hull, ten feet thick. Reading hard burn engines aft, maneuvering thrusters fore and aft. Picking up signs of radioactive decay on what looks like the keel."

"Nukes?" Spadt asked.

"That or a reactor," Jones said, "but I doubt they'd mount their engine on the outside of the ship."

Clayton stroked his chin thoughtfully. Humanity hadn't used nuclear warfare since fleeing Earth. That had, fortunately, limited humanity's destructive capabilities during the corporate war, but it gave the aliens an edge here. Clayton was limited to smaller warheads and a complement of independent firing platforms. What lasers *Trafalgar* had were a huge energy drain and heat danger, and as such were primarily used for point defense. Additionally, Clayton didn't want to commit the small craft until he had a better idea of the alien vessels' short-range defenses.

"Can you give me anything else on their armament?"

"Nothing definitive on scans, sir." Jones said, shaking his head.

"Are we close enough for a visual?"

"Not yet, sir."

"Computer generated schematic then."

"Aye, sir. Formulating... done."

"Put it up front." The blank space in the window above the helm and operations stations flickered and turned white. On the empty background sat a strange object. It was rounded, as if someone had taken a quarter section from a steel globe and scooped out the inside. The front rose a short way before the face sloped upward and inward. The diagram rotated, revealing four stiff phalanges that pulled apart from each other and stretched from the cupped main section of the ship. They reminded Clayton of the ridges on a rooster's comb. The diagram continued to rotate, revealing that the ridges were not singular protrusions, but extended sections of the ship that wrapped around the entire back side. It was an odd design, but elegant.

"How big is that ship?"

"One point two kilometers, stem to stern."

"Which part is the stern?" Spadt asked. It was a question no self-respecting sailor would've thought they'd ask, but no one expected to see a ship that looked like this either.

Cohen stepped forward, out of the mission pod. "I think it's safe to say that it was fabricated in space, whichever end is the front. There's no way that could've launched from a planet's surface."

Castaño interrupted any further speculation. "Sir, launch detected! It's coming straight for us!"

Clayton was on his feet instantly, standing at the rail, hands automatically gripping it. "Jones! Get a bead on that object with the PD grid and get me an analysis of it, ASAP!" Jones set to work, and Clayton returned his attention to Castaño. "Lieutenant Castaño, time to impact?"

"Two minutes at current acceleration." Clayton frowned. That was too long. Even at the beginning of the war, PD grids were more than sophisticated enough to target and destroy warheads in under two minutes. They had to be; the technology had been developed originally for the purpose of navigating asteroid fields safely. Part of him hoped that due to how lightly armed the *Erikson* had been, the aliens might be underestimating the heavier vessels. Clayton had been in enough battles to know better. This was probably a feint, or they were testing *Trafalgar*.

"Captain, the torpedo is carrying an explosive payload," Jones said. "It appears to be small, but there's only so much I can tell about the yield."

"Activate the grid and ready port missile pods, Jones." Clayton pushed his shoulders back and forced himself to let go of the rail and clasp his hands behind his back. "Castaño, once the warhead detonates, swing starboard and bring us closer. Continue to monitor the enemy vessels for further launches. Commander Spadt, I need more eyes on the tactical situation. Get me long range scans. I want to know if there's anything else out there. Advise me of significant ship movements. Dixon, I want your eyes there too, barring significant changes in ship operations."

Clayton's crew set about his orders and Clayton released his hands and pulled down the cuffs of his uniform. Until he could determine what the aliens were really up to, he would steer into the feint. He tapped the rail, and it brought up a holographic display of the alien ship on his right. It certainly was a strange vessel.

"Missile destroyed, captain," Jones said.

Clayton nodded. "Thank you, lieutenant. Move us into firing position, Castaño. Jones, fire once we're in effective range. Spadt, what's the situation with the other ships?"

"*Tovey* is between us and *Nile*, pushing past the orbital path of the outer moon. I'm reading two warhead detonations between the close enemy vessel and the *Tovey*. One detonation between the far ship and the *Nile*. The *Nile*'s still in the moon's gravity." Clayton frowned. Staying within the sphere of a planetary body's gravity limited maneuverability and removed an avenue of retreat. What was she doing?

"Sir, detecting multiple launches from the nearby ship!"

Clayton returned his attention to his own engagement, cursing himself for getting distracted. "Take them as they come, Jones. Castaño, are we within effective range?"

"Coming up on our port side in ten seconds, sir."

"Jones?" Clayton looked at his tactical officer, whose hands were flying around on his console.

"PD grid is mopping up the enemy missiles and ours are ready."

"Fire at will. Dixon, show me port side." The sideways mounting of the bridge was an interesting design feature of the Nelson-class. Full protection from port, complete vulnerability from starboard. It also necessitated the use of cameras for anything blocked by the port side. The clear glass above the front stations turned black for a moment, then showed the dark alien vessel. Moments later, pin-pricks of light illuminated at a number of points on the ship's hull. Clayton settled into his chair.

"Reading five solid hits," Jones said. "Our other missiles were neutralized sir. The ship's going to pass under us."

"What kind of damage did we do?" Spadt looked from Jones to Clayton.

"Looks like our missiles breached the enemy vessel, but the damage seems to be contained."

"Tough ship. Continue on this heading, Castaño, and prepare to pitch down and roll. I want to get them in our sights again so we can hit them with the port missiles again. Spadt, sitrep on the rest of the battle."

"*Tovey* is running out and around the other alien vessel, which is between her and *Nile*. Reading minimal damage to *Nile* and the enemy vessel. Sir, recommend we concentrate fire on the other ship. Eliminate it and then we can move as a unit against the survivor."

"Negative, commander." Clayton shook his head. "Judging from their armament thus far Villeneuve and Amin can take that ship. Let's just make sure they don't get a nasty surprise from our target." Just as Clayton finished speaking the ship rocked, and a deep rumble followed it. Clayton gripped his armrests and managed to keep himself from being thrown from his seat.

"Dixon! Damage report! Jones, what hit us?"

"Reading exterior hull breaches on all decks, sections W–Z port side. No interior breaches," Dixon said.

"I'm not sure, sir," Jones said. "Nothing came up on scans."

"Mines?" Spadt mused. "The PD grid would have picked up and dealt with anything moving at significant velocity."

Clayton nodded. "Must be. Dixon, evacuate those sections and alert our other ships of the possibility of mines. Advise them to avoid flying in the wake of the alien ships. Castaño, take that into consideration for future maneuvers."

"Already on it, sir. We're coming around on them."

"Get us into firing range. Jones, can you target sections we've already damaged?"

Jones wiped his brow. "I think so. Yes sir, within a hundred meters."

"That'll do, lieutenant. Prepare to fire port missiles."

"Aye, sir."

"Castaño, where are we?"

"Coming alongside now."

"Show me." The screen above Castaño lit up with a view of the alien ship. It looked largely undamaged. Clayton felt apprehension clawing up the walls of his stomach. That ship had opened a third of his port side. A second hit in the same section and it would depressurize. Meanwhile, the alien ship floated on, seemingly unconcerned with its own damage.

"Coming into range, captain."

Clayton fixed Jones with a hard look. "Fire as she bears, lieutenant."

"Aye, sir. Firing." The alien ship glided right on the screen. The steel blue metal glinted in the light of the system's sun. Then, small explosions broke the serene image. The first several ignited away from the ship, caught by an invisible defense grid. Then, a number hit the side of the ship. A few of these sustained themselves and grew outward in long plumes before dousing suddenly. Clayton felt a surge of animalistic satisfaction as he watched. The fire was interacting with oxygen—an interior breach. They had done real damage.

"Jones, ready starboard pods. Castaño, roll us."

"Captain, they're returning fire!" Jones looked at Clayton.

"Brace for impact. Let's hope the grid is up for the challenge." Clayton bared his teeth, gripping his chair's armrests. He was betting on a small salvo. If it was anything but, *Trafalgar* was going to take serious damage and the bridge stood a good chance of being breached, even with its armored shell. At this range, there was only so much the PD grid could do. Clayton turned his chair to the right and watched as the alien ship came into view. "Jones, fire on my mark."

"Aye, sir." The alien ship drew closer to being on a level plane with *Trafalgar* and Clayton could see explosions filling the space between the two ships.

"Fire!"

"Missiles away."

"Full to port!" The alien ship began to shrink in Clayton's view and the first of the alien torpedoes breached the PD grid. The bridge shook again, and Clayton was launched sideways out of his chair, over the armrest. Instinctively, he braced himself for the impact. He landed hard on his right hand and pain shot through it. Before he could recover from the fall, the ship shook with another impact and Clayton was thrown right and rolled into the railing that separated his level from that of his operations and flight officers. When the shaking stopped, Clayton pulled himself up on the railing with his left hand. Glancing around the room, Clayton saw that he wasn't the only one to fall out of his chair. Fortunately, everyone looked to be alright.

"Status report."

Below Clayton, Dixon coughed and pulled herself back into her seat. "Exterior breaches on decks one through three, starboard side, sections P–T and on decks three through six, sections B–E." Clayton let out a sigh of relief and cringed as he brushed his right hand against his side. He held in a groan, gritting his teeth. Something was broken.

"Evacuate the appropriate sections. Jones, what's the status of the enemy ship?"

Jones wasn't looking at his console. "Disabled, I think. Take a look for yourself, captain." Clayton looked to where the lieutenant was pointing. The alien ship was still visible, but it drifted, seeming devoid of control. Satisfaction threatened to burst from Clayton's chest, but he held it in.

"It could be a trap," Spadt said.

Clayton turned to look at him. "My thoughts precisely, commander. Castaño, move us away, half ahead. Commander Spadt, what's the situation on the other front?" Spadt tapped on his console a few times before looking back to Clayton.

"It appears to have been resolved, captain, but the other ship could be lying in wait as well. *Tovey's* lost propulsion, but *Nile* appears to be in good shape."

Clayton nodded and returned to his chair. "Commander Dixon, open a channel to Admiral Villeneuve."

"Aye, sir."

Villeneuve's voice crackled through the bridge. "Captain Clayton. We got the bastards, but my ship's in rough shape. Long range scans are out. How go things on your side?"

"We took some damage, but the enemy vessel appears to be incapacitated, sir. They might still have something up their sleeve."

"Noted. Get over here and cover the *Nile* while Amin takes on my wounded."

"On our way, admiral. Clayton out." He nodded to Castaño. "Take us in, lieutenant. Remember the mine trails."

"Aye, sir." The ship rotated and started off toward the bright moon. It hadn't gone far when Jones stood up from his console suddenly.

"Captain, reading massive radiation from the alien ship!"

"Give me a visual!" Clayton instinctively gripped his armrests, grimacing as pain throbbed through his arm. He ignored it. The screen flickered. At first Clayton didn't see anything different. Then the view magnified, and he saw twisted pieces of metal flying away from the center.

"Did they just..." Cohen stepped up behind Clayton's chair.

"Yes. They detonated their nuke or power source. Self-destruct."

"Sir, we're getting a hail from the *Nile*."

"Put it through, commander."

Amin appeared on the left screen. "Captain Clayton, the alien vessel over here just blew itself up. Our ships are fine. What's your status?"

"Same as yours. The alien ship detonated, but we were clear. We're on our way to rendezvous with you and the admiral."

"Understood. Amin out."

Cohen was at the railing ahead of Clayton now, still staring at the display of the broken alien ship. "Surely they knew we were out of their blast radius."

Spadt shook his head. "Maybe they didn't want us to board them or salvage any of their technology."

Clayton stared at the wreckage of the alien ship and shook his head. It was too much like playing chess with Amin. They were missing something. "Even then, commander, why not wait and try to take us with them? This way they accomplished nothing but their own destruction."

CHAPTER XV

Kobayashi unbuckled herself from the navigator's seat and gave Allred a tap on the shoulder. Allred looked back at her and gave her a thumbs up. With a nod, Kobayashi got up and walked back from the cockpit and opened the hatch that led to the back of the transport.

"Feel heavy, Mithril?" She stepped into the troop hold, looking at her team. Lincoln and Buchanan sat next to each other, blue and gold, helmets already on and sealed. Fegan sat with Vang. Nearest her were Conroy and Butler. All still with white armor. If she hadn't known who was where before she stepped back there, she wouldn't have had any idea.

"Hell yeah, I do, major. How many Gs we pulling?" Conroy said.

"One point one-five, specialist, and you'd better get used to it." Kobayashi placed a hand on his shoulder. "It isn't Allred's flying. That gravity you're feeling is all Geneva's. She's a big lady."

"Shit." Fitz looked at Garcia. "If something happens and you can't walk, I ain't carrying you, Gunny." There was a resounding chuckle. Kobayashi saw Buchanan's helmet tilt up, though Lincoln didn't budge.

Holland laughed. "*There's* a big lady for you."

"Watch out or I'll sit on you," Garcia said.

"That's enough chatter," Kobayashi said. She stood in front of the squad now, and they looked up at her, ready to be briefed. "When we hit the ground, Orange team will stay with the shuttle. We don't know anything about the local wildlife or vegetation and I don't want anything getting on the ship."

"You kidding me, major? I was hoping to do some exploring," Fitz said.

Fegan answered for Kobayashi. "Quit whining, Fitz. Now you don't have to worry about carrying Garcia anywhere. We get the easy part of the job, barring territorial, bulletproof octopeds or some other monster."

"You sure know how to make a guy feel better."

Kobayashi pressed on with her briefing. "Nearest LZ to the source of the signal is a clearing about a kilometer out, so Purple and Green are going to have to hoof it and there's a decent chance that any survivors may not be in the immediate vicinity anyway, since they crashed here almost two months ago. Any number of things might have forced them away from the crash site. In the event that we don't find anyone, we'll radio back and Orange team will start putting together a base camp for further searches and any other operations Captain Clayton approves down here. Questions?" Kobayashi glanced around the team and Hale spoke up.

"You said further searches. How long are we going to be down here looking?"

Kobayashi held back a shrug. "Best guess, three or four days. Command didn't give a timeline with our orders. I guess it depends on what happens with the ETs. With a little luck, we'll find the survivors within the next few hours. Standard emergency procedure is to keep close to the transmitter. Hopefully they tried to follow it." The shuttle shook and Kobayashi lurched, hand automatically reaching up to grab a hold above the seats. The red alert light at the front of the cabin lit up.

Allred's voice came over the speaker. "We're about five minutes out, team. Suggest you strap in; it's going to be choppy for the next couple minutes."

Kobayashi nodded and lowered herself into an empty seat next to Fegan. "Helmets on. We don't know what kind of pathogens might be floating around down there."

"Lock and load, people!" Fegan turned to Kobayashi as he secured his helmet. "Surprised you're keeping Allred out of the fight. She's got a good head on her shoulders. She'd do well in the field."

"Agreed. I'm leaving her here because I want the engines hot. We've got a couple qualified medics here, but if the survivors are in a bad enough way, I want to be ready to go."

"Understood, major."

The shuttle settled into a nervous quiet and Kobayashi took the opportunity to observe her team. Hale and Larson sat next to each other rigid. Vang inspected his rifle carefully, while Hammond bounced his weapon on his lap and Butler drummed his fingers on his knee. The others talked in low voices. Kobayashi saw Garcia's chest convulsing in stifled laughter, while Conroy shook his head. Kobayashi was unsure of the team as a whole. The Exos and NFs seemed to trust each other, but with the shakeup after Johansen and the addition of Hale and Larson, Kobayashi didn't know what other conflicts might present themselves. Time would tell and she would handle them as they came.

A buzz sounded throughout the compartment and the team stiffened as the shuttle sharpened its descent, pressing them down into and back against their seats. The shuttle began to shake. Kobayashi closed her eyes and breathed in deeply. She held the breath for a moment, then released it.

After a long time like that, Kobayashi felt the shuttle decelerate, the inertia pushing her into her seat lessening. Then, with a *thummm*, the shuttle pressed onto solid ground, tilted slightly forward and settled. As Kobayashi opened her eyes, Garcia's voice crackled through the coms. "Nice landing, lieutenant. Most of the time, it seems like historic firsts involve more crashing."

"Thanks, José, but to be fair, this wasn't a first. Remember that escape pod we're here to check on? And that probably did crash."

"Ah, that doesn't count."

"Cut the chatter." Kobayashi unclipped herself and stepped carefully onto the inclined floor. The design might be good for making landings gentler, but it was still a pain to walk on. "Orange, Green, secure the area outside. Larson, Garcia grab trauma kits." The team bustled around the compartment, retrieving their gear.

Kobayashi pulled her pack from the storage area above the seats and retrieved a handgun from the rack near the ramp at the back as it descended on its hydraulics. Pulling back the lever, she ensured that it was empty before grabbing a few heat sinks for her weapons. She grabbed a stock and strap, attaching them before inserting a heat sink and slinging the weapon over her shoulder.

The members of Orange and Green teams, led by Fegan while Allred ran through post-flight in the cockpit, led the way out of the shuttle, rifles held to their shoulders as they surveyed the area. Kobayashi and the rest of Mithril followed them out. Fegan and his men spread out, stepping into the forest while the others waited, eyes flicking around the clearing. It was dark enough that Kobayashi couldn't make out much before she turned her night vision on. The grass grew as high as mid-shin before flopping about. The trees were short and gnarled, with some kind of speckled coloring. They bore large leaves that Kobayashi found reminiscent of palm or frond leaves. She saw no sign of fauna in the area. If animals of some kind existed here, they had probably been scared off by the shuttle's approach.

One by one, members of the recon teams returned from various points in the forest. Thanks to the motion tracker that highlighted them as they approached from the forest, Kobayashi saw them well before they reemerged into the clearing. As the last group returned, she saw Allred descending the ramp in her rearview. Fegan stepped up to her.

"All teams reporting all clear, major."

"Understood, Fegan." Kobayashi nodded and turned to face Allred as she approached. "Lieutenant, have your team prepare the area for base camp assembly, but don't unload anything yet. We'll check in every fifteen minutes."

"Yes, ma'am."

Kobayashi looked back at the rest of the team, "Green, Purple, let's move out. We're headed due..." Kobayashi checked her heads-up display, only to realize it had no compass. Even if it had, it would have had to be calibrated to Geneva's magnetic field to be useful. That was something to bring up to the techs. Fortunately, there was a transmitter on the Coon, if they got turned around. She gestured past the shuttle. "Towards the distress signal. Green, you're on point."

Nods were given around the huddle and the group broke up. Hale strode past Kobayashi, flanked by Garcia and Butler, with Holland following. Kobayashi stepped in behind Holland and Vang fell in beside her, leaving Hammond and Larson on rear guard. There was no reason to suspect danger, but Kobayashi and her team had enough experience to know that a lack of knowledge was no defense against the unexpected. They would hold this formation and keep their wits about them.

As they strode into the forest, the team kept itself well spaced, the lead pair watching forward, while Kobayashi and the others in the center scanned their flanks. Hammond and Larson alternated with each other between watching the back and walking forward comfortably. The deeper they went into the forest, the more disconcerted Kobayashi felt. The tree trunks were all twisted and contorted in an unreasonable manner. Often, they intertwined with each other. Branches stuck out as low as shoulder level, forcing the team to duck under them. Larson and Garcia, both over six feet tall, spent about as much time bent over as they did standing. For the most part, the trees were spaced far enough apart that the team was able to maintain formation and line of sight of each other with little difficulty. The undergrowth was short and scrappy. It seemed that there was little to fill the size profile of a bush; everything was grass or trees.

After several minutes of walking, Kobayashi spoke into her helmet. "VATAS, increase ambient sound volume thirty percent, but keep the team's noise level the same." Her helmet chirped and Kobayashi listened carefully. Nothing changed. There was not a sound to be heard, aside from the muffled footfalls of her team. "VATAS, resume normal audio levels and open comms with Orange team." There was another chirp and a window opened above the roster on Kobayashi's HUD. "Purple to Orange, come in."

"Allred here, major."

Kobayashi exhaled slowly. "Sit-rep, lieutenant."

"All clear, ma'am. We're clearing the area of debris now."

"Good. We're a couple minutes out from the source of the distress signal. Keep me apprised of any changes in the environment."

"Understood ma'am."

"Kobayashi out." The line cut and Kobayashi returned her full attention to the silent forest. A slight shiver shook her body, despite the warm, somewhat muggy atmosphere. The team pushed on quietly, stepping carefully, rifles swiveling, but nothing changed. There were no new sounds and Kobayashi's VATAS highlighted no movement. Finally, she saw a break in the trees and picked up her pace, closing the distance to the front of the team. They paused for a moment, watching the still clearing. Kobayashi tapped Holland's shoulder and he in turn tapped Hale's. Hale nodded and she and Garcia broke cautiously into the open and rotated around a large, oval object in the area: the escape pod.

"Clear!"

"Clear!"

Kobayashi nodded and looked at Vang. "Check the pod. I'm right behind you. Everyone else, establish a perimeter."

"Yes, ma'am."

The team spread out and Kobayashi followed Vang to the lip of the pod. It sat at an acute angle, half toppled, held partially upright by an extremely heavy base buried a foot or two into the ground. The hatch into it had been blown off its hinges and the entire white capsule was stained with smoke streaks. Vang stared into the pod for a moment before wrapping the strap of his rifle around one arm.

"Going in."

Kobayashi stepped up beside him and pointed her own rifle into the pod. "Copy. Go." Vang climbed awkwardly into the tilted pod and pressed into the darkness. Kobayashi waited for a moment, able to see his silhouette highlighted in green. Then a light came on in the pod, illuminating a scorched white interior, empty, except for Vang.

"Clear!" Kobayashi sighed and lowered her rifle as he returned to the entrance of the pod. He hopped down, shaking his head slightly. "No sign that anyone was inside."

Kobayashi frowned behind her helmet. "Except that it was open. Those doors aren't designed to open with a breeze."

"So much for staying with the pod."

Kobayashi shrugged. "Maybe they set up camp someplace near—"

"Back off! Back off! Who the hell are you?"

Kobayashi and Vang sprung away from the pod, rifles raised to their shoulders. They hurried around the pod to where Hale and Larson stood, rifles pointing into the forest. Kobayashi stopped and placed a hand on Vang's shoulder. He looked at her and she shook her head, watching as Larson lowered his rifle and laid it on the ground.

"Hey, it's alright. We're J-REF—marines. We came here to rescue you."

Kobayashi looped around until she could see what was going on. A man dressed in leaves stood with a tall woman slumped against him. She looked faint, white as a sheet, despite the two distinct skin tones on her. The man's shoulders relaxed slightly, then the woman's head lolled to the side, and he tensed again.

"Soldiers?" He paused and looked behind him and looked forward again, eyes darting from one marine to the next, before making a decision. "You've got to help us. I don't know how far away they are."

"Alright, we'll help you, just take it easy."

Kobayashi stepped forward. "We'll take you back to our ship." She took a good look at the woman, whose eyes dropped as she snapped her neck up, trying to stay awake. "She doesn't look so good. We should get her on a stretcher."

The man nodded quickly. "Right. Of course."

Kobayashi looked back at the rest of the team that had assembled around them. "Garcia, break out a stretcher. Larson you're on the other end. Vang, Hale, I want you two to head back to the shuttle, make sure the path is clear. Tell Allred we've found the survivors."

"Aye, ma'am." The two nodded to her and moved out. Kobayashi looked back at the man.

"You are the only survivors?"

The man looked at her, eyebrows creased before replying. "Yes, of course." Kobayashi maintained eye contact while Garcia assembled the stretcher. His gaze didn't waver and the arm he had wrapped around the woman's waist tightened slightly.

"I'm Major Kobayashi. This is Chief Warrant Officer Larson, in the gold, and Gunnery Sergeant Garcia. They're both qualified corpsmen. They'll take good care of your friend until we can get to the surgeon on *Trafalgar*."

The man nodded. "Thanks." He swallowed, then added, "I'm Fred Cooper."

"Larson." Garcia nodded towards the stretcher.

"Aye." Larson nodded and adjusted his rifle as he stepped up to it.

Cooper started forward, dragging the woman with him. Kobayashi stepped forward and helped him lower her onto the stretcher. Once she was there and stable, Kobayashi stood and gestured first to Butler and Hammond, then back in the direction of the shuttle. They nodded and moved back into the forest. Garcia checked the bandage on the woman's wound and nodded.

"Damned if I know what this material is, but it seems to make a decent bandage," Garcia said. He squatted and together with

Larson picked up the stretcher. Cooper hovered nearby as they started on their way. Kobayashi and Holland took up the rear guard. There was no sign of motion. Whatever had been chasing Cooper and his friend had either lost the scent or scattered at the sight of Kobayashi's team.

"What's her name?" Kobayashi watched Larson and Cooper talk in her rearview.

"Shar'hre."

"Sherry?"

"No. Shaar-Hree."

Larson nodded. "Shar'hre. Got it. What was chasing you?"

Before Cooper had a chance to respond, Vang's voice cut through on a line. "Bad news, major. *Trafalgar*'s not responding to hails."

Kobayashi grimaced. "Tell Allred to keep trying and to warm up the engines. This woman's in pretty bad shape and whatever hurt her is still out there. If *Trafalgar*'s nearby, we need the surgeon."

"Yes, ma'am. Vang out."

"You're kidding? Here?"

Kobayashi returned her attention to Larson and Cooper's conversation, ducking under a branch. As she straightened, the ground rolled beneath her and she stumbled. She glanced at Holland who had one of his arms out to steady himself. The ground rolled again, harder and Kobayashi had to catch herself on a tree to keep herself upright. In her rearview, she saw Garcia and Larson stumble, the stretcher wobbling dangerously. Cooper reached to steady it.

"Don't worry. These quakes don't last long, and they don't get much worse than this."

"You mean these are common?" Kobayashi could hear Larson's clenched teeth in his voice.

"Every few days, it seems."

"Alright, set her down." Kobayashi braced her back against the tree. "We'll wait until these quakes subside. We don't want to drop her and aggravate her injuries."

"Affirmative, major."

The ground continued to shake, and Kobayashi carefully lowered herself to the ground. "VATAS, page Allred."

There was a chirp and Allred responded. "Allred here. Is everything alright, major?"

"Yes, we're just waiting out the quake. One of the survivors says they don't usually last too long. Where are we on comms with *Trafalgar*?"

"Still no response. And I'm not picking up its transponder either. They could have changed their orbit or moved out of range of the Coon's transmitters."

"Understood. Keep trying. Kobayashi out." The line cut and Kobayashi swallowed the bile rising in her throat. The team waited uneasily as the quake continued. Despite the growing throb in her skull, Kobayashi noticed that Cooper, unlike everyone else, wasn't bracing against anything. He simply sat on the ground, rocking next to the stretcher. She watched as he steadied himself with his fingertips when the quake got the better of him. He seemed unbothered by them. Kobayashi couldn't tell if that was because he was so concerned about the woman or if he had simply acclimatized that well to the environment.

After several, long minutes, the shaking subsided and Kobayashi stood and surveyed the area, breathing deeply. "Alright, let's go, people." The others had already been rising to their feet and it was only a few moments before they were moving through the trees in formation again. There was still no sign of animal life and no sound aside from those made by the team. Larson and Cooper did not resume their conversation. Finally, they came into the clearing where Orange team and the two Kobayashi had sent ahead waited. Allred was nowhere to be seen. She was likely in the cockpit running through preflight.

Fegan saw the team and approached Kobayashi. "Major, Allred's made contact with *Trafalgar*. Apparently, the ETs showed up and there was a battle. They had to leave orbit but are en route now."

Kobayashi sighed and nodded. "Good." She glanced around the clearing. "A bit small for a base camp. If we have to come back, we can probably find a better place. Let's get loaded up."

Fegan nodded. "Understood, major."

Garcia and Larson carried the stretcher up the ramp and the rest of the squad was soon strapping into their seats. Garcia and Larson transferred Shar'hre from the stretcher onto a cot that pulled out of the floor. It had a built-in gyroscope to hold the bed even despite being at an angle to the floor.

Once Shar'hre was in and everyone was strapped in their seats, Kobayashi moved up into the cockpit and lowered herself into the navigator's seat. "All aboard. Let's go."

Allred nodded and flipped a couple switches above them. "Yes, ma'am. Beginning liftoff sequence." Kobayashi strapped in and glanced over her shoulder, into the passenger compartment. As the door slid shut behind her, she thought she saw a hand raising itself from the cot between the rows of soldiers. She exhaled and looked forward again. The engines roared to life and the shuttle tilted forward and began to rise. As it did so, the leaves of the trees in front of the shuttle blew upward, sending a shimmering wave through the leaves of the forest.

Fred stared out the porthole at the tiny, twinkling stars. After being released from the medical bay and told that he would be notified regarding Shar'hre's status as soon as there was something of note, he'd asked if there were any windows on the ship. The orderly had guided him here and Fred had been staring out at the vast canvas of space ever since. It might have been twenty minutes. It could have been an hour. All he could do was think about Shar'hre.

Something of note. How much more impersonal could they get? Fred hadn't approved of either military during the war. The fact that they had been merged instead of disbanded continued to irk him, despite the fact that without them, he and Shar'hre would have been captured. Ends did not justify means. Maybe there was something to all the propaganda about the merger healing the wounds of war. Still, they had come heavily armed and dressed head to toe in armor unlike anything he'd ever seen. Fred's thoughts were interrupted by a voice behind his shoulder.

"Calming, isn't it?"

Fred turned to see a man in dress whites, one arm in a sling. He was shorter than Fred, something that Fred was still getting used to after his time among the giants down on Galjain. Or Geneva, as the Renovamen called it.

"Yeah, it can be." Fred noted the monoplane on the man's shoulder. "Are you the captain of this ship?"

The man smiled and extended his good hand. "Aye. Captain Jim Clayton. And you're Fred Cooper."

Fred shook Clayton's hand. "How is Shar'hre?"

Clayton removed his cover and fiddled with it. "Your friend is in post-op now, Mister Cooper. My surgeon tells me she should be fine, but he says that there were a few irregularities in her anatomy, and she wasn't on the *Erikson*'s crew manifest, so there was nothing to reference in regard to that."

Fred exhaled, shoulders dropping. Then he scoffed, almost chuckling. "That would be because she wasn't aboard the *Erikson*." Fred watched with a certain satisfaction as Clayton's eyebrows scrunched together then slowly parted.

"You mean—"

"Yes. She's from Geneva. There's a whole culture down there. Maybe more than one. My hypothesis is that there was another exodus from Earth, separate from the one that brought our ancestors to Zoar."

Clayton shook his head. "And you were with these people for two months?"

"Is that how long it's been?" Fred looked up at the ceiling. He hadn't known how to gauge time on Galjain as it compared to Zoar, aside from some conversion equation one of the *Erikson's* scientists had told him shortly after they'd arrived in orbit. But he hadn't thought about that since the *Erikson* went up in flames. It hadn't really mattered once the Meltesh found him. Turning his gaze from the ceiling he found Clayton looking at him expectantly. "Yes. They found my pod after it came down. Shar'hre was no'ihrah who nursed me back to health."

Clayton rubbed his chin. "How did they react to you?"

Fred grinned sheepishly, not making direct eye contact with Clayton. "They thought I was some kind of messenger from their deities as far as I can tell."

"I hope you didn't play into that." Clayton had stiffened, arms dropping to his side.

Fred's face flushed. "If I did, it was only because I couldn't do much else, captain. I lived down there for two months, remember? It's not like I could know what my actions meant at first." They stared at each other for a few moments, while Fred felt any sympathetic thoughts he might have begun to entertain regarding Clayton and the military slipping away until Clayton broke the silence.

"We need to get out ahead of this. What do you think about returning to Zoar?"

Fred's jaw tightened. Who did this guy think he was? Fred was under no obligation to accept orders from him. "To be honest, captain, I'd rather go back to the surface. The Meltesh are a genuine people, even in their violence."

"And I'd like them to remain genuine, Mister Cooper. As such, I'm glad you're not in too much of a hurry to go home. You're the only person with experience regarding these people. With you here, acting as a go between and translator for us, things should go much smoother for us."

What was Clayton getting at? "I'm not interested in representing the Navy."

"Good. I expected as much."

Fred frowned. "Then what do you want, captain?"

Clayton took a deep breath. "I want to keep these people from being conquered and all the suffering that comes with it." He looked at Fred. "I read your file. I know you protested the war and I know that you earned a full bachelor's degree in Castellano Spanish. You must have some idea of what kind of damage a superior force like that of the Renovamen could do to people still using spears and swords. I want to prevent that."

Fred's mind raced. "And how do I know you mean that?"

Clayton looked forward, out the porthole again. "Beyond having this conversation, there's not much I can do to prove it right now, is there? You'll have to trust me. Otherwise, I can send you over to one of the other ships and you can go back to Zoar. I'll return your friend to the surface and do my best to navigate the Meltesh without your help."

Fred stared at Clayton. Back to Zoar? And leave the Meltesh alone with three JREF ships in orbit? That would require infinitely more trust than staying where he could track Clayton's actions.

"No. I'm staying."

ACKNOWLEDGEMENTS

As a reader, I always appreciate when the author attempts to give credit where it's due, although it is an impossible task to fully carry off, given how intricately one's life intertwines with their thoughts. Nevertheless, I would be remiss to not even attempt to acknowledge the people who have most fully affected the writing of this book in particular.

As an eight year old child, I discovered my passion for writing by emulating my brother, so to him I must give thanks first. After him, I must thank my sisters, who were the first people to read the first completed draft of not only this book but three that are to follow. The road of a writer is a lonely one and having people read hundreds of pages of drafts is a great source of validation.

Speaking of validation, I must also thank Erin Saldin, Miranda Morgan, Robert Stubblefield, Dee McNamer, Chris Dombrowski and all of my fellows in the various workshops they led that I was a member of. When I first arrived at the University of Montana I would have been a disappointment to my eight-year-old self. My aspirations of writing were on a backburner and I lacked the drive to pursue them in a serious manner. When I submitted my first piece, I was relieved and even giddy to find enthusiasm and encouragement from my workshop. From there on out, regardless of whether I was writing fiction or nonfiction, working on this story or another, I was much more motivated and confident. With each workshop I took, I was exposed to writing I would never have experienced otherwise and advice and perspective I couldn't have found elsewhere and all of this contributed to a certainty that this was a path I could and would continue down.

I would also like to thank my editor Martin Hill for all the work he did in the nitty gritty, from correcting commas and colons to enlightening me on aspects of military etiquette. Thanks also to Phillip Dannels for the excellent cover art.

In a more general sense, I'd like to thank the creators of all the many stories that have entertained, inspired and provoked me to think. Likewise, thanks to all the many friends I've had throughout my life. I am grateful for the ways in which each of you stimulated my mind and imagination, through play or discussion. All the teachers, coaches, bosses and other mentors I've had from kindergarten through college I thank for inspiring me at my best and teaching me tough lessons at my worst.

And of course, thank you, reader. As I mentioned before, it means a great deal to have someone reach the end of my book and if you're reading this, I imagine you have finished the book. I hope you enjoyed it and that you will consider reading the sequel when it becomes available.

Finally, I must thank my parents. Who could be more important to the development of this book than the people responsible for the development of its author? Thank you for supporting me and loving me for all these years.

About the Author

Anders Holmquist was born and raised in western Montana. He attended Frenchtown High School and the University of Montana in Missoula. *Zoar and Geneva* is his first novel.